The Dying Man . . .

He'd crawled out of the cruel sun, but it hadn't done him much good. Someone had stripped him to the buff. Then they'd cut off his nose and eyelids.

Then they'd peeled the soles of his feet to turn him loose on the hot desert sands.

Stringer protested, "We can't just leave him here like this!"

"Why not?" asked Pancho Villa.

LOU CAMERON

STRINGER

AND THE BORDER WAR

CHARTER BOOKS, NEW YORK

STRINGER AND THE BORDER WAR

A Charter Book / published by arrangement with the author

PRINTING HISTORY
Charter Original / April 1989

ISBN: 1-55773-182-9

Charter Books are published by The Berkley Publishing Group,
200 Madison Avenue, New York, N.Y. 10016.
The name "Charter" and the "C" logo are trademarks belonging
to Charter Communications Inc.

PRINTED IN THE UNITED STATES OF AMERICA

10 9 8 7 6 5 4 3 2 1

CHAPTER
ONE

They'd been told to lay for him on the southwest corner of Montgomery and Market. That meant the son of a bitch who'd sent them knew the way Stringer usually walked to work from his hired digs on Rincon Hill. There were six of them. That meant the son of a bitch was serious. They began by falling in around Stringer as he was crossing Market and shoving him facedown across the streetcar tracks, in front of a rush hour streetcar bound for the Oakland Ferry. That didn't work. Stringer turned his dive to the tracks into a forward somersault, just in time, and was up and running by the time steel flanges were chewing hell out of the fashionable straw skimmer he'd just bought to go with the business suit he had to wear in town.

He knew better than to run far. As the hired thugs chased after him, he spotted a swell niche in a cast-iron storefront and spun to face all six of them with his back protected. That still left the rest of him up for grabs. His only consolation was that six guys tended to get in each other's way as they all tried to knock his block off at once, and he knew the coppers wouldn't stand for much of a brawl in downtown Frisco during the morning rush unless the fix was in.

The fix was in. The tough young newspaper man and

1

erstwhile cowhand put the one with the blackjack on the pavement with a left hook, and crippled the one with the knife with a kick to the kneecap, by the time he'd lost one sleeve of his jacket and felt one eye swell shut. But the four left were better boxers, which was, no doubt, why they were still left, and where, for Chrissake, were the fucking coppers?

With more elbowroom to throw punches from, one of the grimly silent attackers landed a right cross that made Stringer see stars and taste a little blood. He somehow managed a counterpunch. But there wasn't as much steam in it as his brain had directed his fist to deliver. His legs were starting to feel like empty rubber boots under him. He knew, even as he kept punching back, that he'd be going down any time, now, and he knew they meant to stomp to ten and then some.

But, just as Stringer caught one punch with an elbow and another with his floating ribs, another gent joined the party to grab two of the thugs by the scruffs of their necks and smash their heads together before he demolished the face of a third with a ham-sized but rock-hard fist. Stringer threw a left hook at the sole survivor, sucker-punching him as he stared in horror at the beefy giant who'd just demolished his pals. That left all six on the pavement in various stages of moaning disrepair. But before Stringer could fall down beside them to wait for the paddy wagon, his moose-like savior dragged him around the corner by one arm, suggesting, "You need the services of a druggist I know as much as you need a morning in Police Court, Laddy Buck."

Stringer didn't argue. For, aside from the logic of his old pal's suggestion, nobody ever argued with Gentleman Jim Corbett about *anything* if it could possibly be avoided.

San Francisco's answer to John L. Sullivan was now pushing forty and he'd put on even more weight after being retired from the ring by Battling Bob Fitzsimmons in '97. But, as he'd just shown, he was still a fine broth of a boyo against mere thugs of mortal clay.

As Gentleman Jim steered the equally tall but much slimmer Stringer around a beer dray, to haul him across the side street to the druggist he had in mind, Stringer felt obliged to mutter, "That was neighborly as hell of you, Champ, but I sure hope you're just passing through town. I can't even tell you who sent those bastards, and their boss, whoever he may be, isn't going to be happy about what you just did."

Gentleman Jim grinned wolfishly to reply, "Let's hope they come after us again before I have to check out of the Saint Francis tonight, then. Lucky for you, this evening will be me last performance at the Orpheum. I told you the last time we met on the Oakland Ferry that I'm on the same bill with Cole Younger and Frank James. They lecture the youth of today on the wages of sin, and I warn them never to be leading with your right. It's a grand shiner you'll be having if we don't fix it fast, and I see you stopped a stiff one with your upper lip as well. Have you tried your front teeth of late, Laddy Buck?"

As they entered the hole-in-the-wall drugstore to be enveloped in medicinal smells and dim light, Stringer ran a stiff tongue hard over the backs of his front teeth to feel with considerable relief that none seemed loose, after all.

A gnomish little druggist came out of the gloom at them with a suspicious expression, recognised Gentleman Jim, then smiled and said, "You sure are hard on sparring partners, Champ. Let's see, now . . . I'd say we have a three leech job on our hands."

The two of them led Stringer into an even smaller back room and sat him on a bentwood chair. As the druggist took a jar of fat, wet-looking leeches from a shelf, Stringer protested he didn't need one on his *mouth*, damnit. But Gentleman Jim growled, "Don't argue with the doc. Would you rather be wandering about for a week with a fat lip, or get it over with here and now? I know a fancy French eatery in New York where people pay good money to be *eating* snails and such. It can't feel half as disgusting to let a slug sip a bit of yourself, right?"

So Stringer submitted. In truth it didn't hurt, and one got used to the cold wet creatures after they'd stuck to your face a few moments. The druggist put two on Stringer's swollen eye and just one to his bruised lip. Stringer could already feel the swelling going down as Gentleman Jim told the druggist about their grand brawl on Market, before turning back to Stringer to ask who they might have been fighting.

"I just told you I don't know, damn it," Stringer muttered from under the bloodsucker on his lip, "I do a lot of features for my paper and you know how sensitive some gents are. Those bully boys could have been sent after me by a water commissioner I exposed a spell back. On the other hand, I've been doing some stuff on a big shot realtor who'd like to move Chinatown to the mud flats north of Hunter's Point, now that the east slopes of Nob Hill have gotten more fashionable."

Gentleman Jim whistled softly and said, "I wish my troupe wasn't booked next week for San Jose. It sounds to me as if you could use a little help, and if Old Cole,

Frank, and me were to pay a little visit to the fine office of that big shot . . ."

"I can't say for sure it's him." Stringer cut in, trying not to smile at the picture, lest the leech on his lip lose its grip.

All three of the slimy buggers were bigger, heavier, and a lot warmer, now. The druggist noticed that, too. He peeled them off and stuck three fresh, hungry ones to Stringer's face as the battered newspaper man muttered, "Aw, shit."

Gentleman Jim told him to shut up and tough it out, adding, "You should have seen how many they put on my face the night I lost to Fitzsimmons. But, by the next day my own mother, at least, could have recognised me. There's nothing like leeching a shiner before it can set purple and green on you. Leeches don't help much once that happens and it's a pain in the ass to have people asking you, weeks later, about the door you walked into."

None of this was fresh news to any Edwardian who led as active a life as Stringer, and as a matter of fact his face was already feeling a lot better. There was something to be said for old-fashioned druggists, even though some fancy new sawbones did hold that treating bruises with live leeches was sort of unsanitary. Stringer's nose for news twitched and inspired him to ask the druggist what he did with leeches after they'd sucked on someone for a spell. The druggist looked blank, then said, "I put 'em back in a jar with a little water and let 'em get hungry some more. Takes 'em a few days before they're fit to use again. Why do you ask?"

Stringer grimaced and said, "Germs. Modern Medicine holds that sickness is spread from one person to the next by germs. So how do you know leech bites can't spread, say, the siph from one of your customers to the next and, by the way, who was the last gent these buggers on my face sucked on?"

The druggist chuckled and said, "As a matter of fact, these particular leeches last enjoyed a good meal on the battered face of a pretty lady. Her husband has a drinking problem. Other than that, she didn't look sick to me."

Gentleman Jim chimed in with, "Leech bites don't spread nothing bad. Take it from one who knows. Considering some of the places I've boxed in me time, by now I'd have come down with the clap and worse if they did."

The three of them laughed, and since the damage had been done, if such treatment was damaging, Stringer submitted to a few rounds with the leeches. When the druggist handed him a mirror to view the results, he smiled and said, "I'll be damned. It worked. Now all I need is a new suit."

Gentleman Jim walked him to a nearby Army & Navy store but didn't go in with him, saying he had to get back to the theatre before an acrobat stole the Flora Dora dancer he was working on. So they shook on it, and as the ex-champ turned to leave Stringer felt obliged to call out, "Hey, Champ—that's one I owe you. I won't forget it."

To which the burly Corbett replied with a shrug, saying, "Aw, go on, Laddy Buck. You'd have done as much for me, wouldn't you?"

Stringer nodded, soberly, and said, "I guess I would have. Why do you suppose guys like us act so foolish, Champ?"

CHAPTER
TWO

When Stringer arrived at the *San Francisco Sun* a little late, he was wearing a blue denim jacket and matching jeans in place of the suit he'd ruined in the fight. As he entered the little frosted glass box they kept Sam Barca in, the crusty, bald feature editor glanced up from his cluttered desk to dryly remark, "I give up, where's your rough rider hat and six-gun, Cowboy?"

Stringer sat down across from Barca and reached for the Bull Durham makings he'd managed to preserve along with his shirt. He said, "I could have *used* my .38, just now. The sissy suit you expect me to wear to this office got torn off me by a gang of Barbary Coast types. Didn't you tell me you covered the story when they cleaned up the Barbary Coast, Sam?"

Barca sighed wistfully and replied, "That was a big mistake. There was a time when all the real villains in town could be found in one place. Tell me about the bunch you just ran into, old son."

Stringer did. When he'd finished, Barca nodded soberly and opined, "I told you there was little reward in sticking up for Chinamen in this town. I don't think I'd be doing either you or Gentleman Jim a favor if I ran what you just told me. Anyone can see they got to a

7

precinct captain at the very least. You'd both better lay low a while."

Stringer began to build his smoke as he replied, "Corbett's leaving town with his vaudeville troupe tonight. I'd be happy to go on home to the Mother Lode country if my Uncle Don's woman, Crazy Aunt Ida, could cook, and I admired being a poor relation. But I can make more money here in 'Frisco by accident than I could ever make in cattle country on purpose, which is why I gave up herding cows to begin with. So . . ."

"I got an out-of-town feature for you." Barca cut in, adding, "I was considering you for it in any case. Didn't you meet up with a border bandito called Francisco Villa while you were covering the demise of Judge Roy Bean a spell back?"

Stringer licked the seam of his straw colored cigarette paper to seal the contents before he nodded and said, "They call him Pancho. He hates us pretty good. But, he made an exception in my case when we both had to shoot it out with the same troop of rurales. Los Rurale's seem to hate everybody. What's old Pancho Villa been up to, now?"

Barca rummaged through the clutter on his desk as he muttered, "You're not going to believe this. I know I don't. But, oh, here we have the tip from the wire service."

Barca scanned the torn-off yellow sheet without offering to show it to Stringer as he said, "Right. The event is to take place just south of Columbus, New Mexico. Ever been there?"

Stringer lit his smoke thoughtfully before he decided, "Just to jerk water. Never got off the train. I suspect they squeeze the boiler water from the cactus all around. Columbus is one dry little town. I'm being mighty complimentary when I call it a town. Didn't know it was on the border, though. The rails have to twist a mite through that stretch of hilly desert. So I'd guess Columbus was a good five miles north of the border, which is only an imaginary line that far west of El Paso."

Barca said, "No matter. This tip is too crazy to be true in the first place and, if there's anything to it, five miles ain't that long a buggy ride. They say the grandstand's being built just north of the border, with a fine view south into the just-as-dismal state of Chihuahua."

Stringer blew a thoughtful smoke ring and stared through it at the older man to reply, "Grandstand? You mean like they're fixing to have a ball game or stock show just south of the border, Sam?" To which Barca replied, in a tone of disgusted disbelief, "Or something indeed. Pancho Villa and his rebels have agreed to hold a public battle with the private army of one Don Luis Terrazas. *Him* we know more about. Terrazas is probably the biggest, and certainly the most hated, ranchero in Chihuahua. Villa keeps stealing his cows and feeding them to poor people like he thinks he's some sort of Mexican Robin Hood. So add it up."

Stringer did, to say, "I can see why they want to have a shoot-out, Sam. But in front of a *grandstand*, at a set time and place? That sounds dumb as hell, even for Mex gunslicks."

Barca nodded and replied, "I never said I admired the way they make war down yonder. It seems a gringo promoter got word the two sides were fixing to have a battle royal in any case. So he propositioned both sides to hold it just south of his grandstand by cutting them both in on the proceeds. Tickets to view a real battle are going at a buck a seat and, of course, they'll make as much again on soda pop and souvenir programs. I hadn't even thought of the hired hacks they'll be running out to the battlefield from the nearest rail stop until you just mentioned it. Unless they've been paid in advance, which I doubt, only the winning side figures to collect from the promoter, of course."

Stringer chuckled dryly and said, "Here's to Yankee ingenuity, then. Sometimes it's tougher to see why the Mexicans seem to hate us so much. But, young Pancho struck me as a pretty slick guerrilla leader, the one time we met. Do you really think he'd go along with such a *loco en la cabeza* notion?"

Barca shrugged and answered, "For money? Why not? You can buy a Mex virgin for less than a Frisco whore demands, and El Presidente Diaz has been selling off the whole country as he's saving up for his retirement."

Stringer brightened and said, "Hey, *there's* a story I know to be true. A rich American widow just bought more than a million acres of Tehuantepec, as a sort of winter home, and had the ten thousand or so families living on it evicted as squatters by Los Rurales. I hear a young Indio called Zapata has been gathering his own rebel army down that way and . . ."

"Nobody cares." Barca cut in, adding, "The Diaz regime is in good with Washington, as well it should be, considering how the Yanqui Dollar is valued by the greedy bastards. There's no news in Mex rebels, as a rule. They've been trying to overthrow Diaz since he seized power back in '76 and, like I said, he *knows* how to get along with *us*. The human interest in this angle about a battle to be held as a public spectacle is that it's sort of amusing as well as unusual, see?"

Stringer scowled and said, "Unusual, yes. Funny, no. I got to see some Spanish-speaking gents die, gutshot, down in Cuba during the War With Spain. They say folks drove out from Washington to view the Battle Of Bull Run, too. Nobody got to laugh much as the boys in blue and gray went down full of minie balls and grape shot, Sam."

Barca shrugged and said, "Slant the story serious, then. I'll still pay space rates and traveling expenses and, while you're out of town, I'll see what I can find out about your torn-up suit. Big shots don't like to send thugs after a reporter once they know his paper's on to 'em. So, what do you say?"

Stringer sighed and got to his feet, saying, "Might as well. I'm as likely to get killed here as there. So I may as well get paid while I'm ducking, right?"

Knowing the time table of the Southern Pacific Coaster by heart, after riding it so often, Stringer knew he had just time to run home and dress right for cactus country before he had to catch his train. In his boarding house on Rincon Hill, he left his new denim outfit on, since it was neater to wear to a social gathering than the similar but badly-weathered denim he usually wore in the field. He hauled on his spurred and tight but well broken-in black Justins. He replaced his shoestring tie with a black sateen kerchief, rolled so that the ends hung down like a tie. He checked his face in the pier glass and saw that while his tanned face looked somewhat the worse for wear, he hadn't grown enough chin whiskers to matter since he'd last shaved. He ran a comb through his light brown hair and put on the old rough rider hat he'd brought back from Cuba. Knowing how sissy the West Coast had gotten since he was a boy, he left his six-gun rig in his gladstone with the other possibles he was toting along. Then he locked the bag, locked his garret room door after him, and headed down the narrow stairs.

As he passed the door of the gal on the second landing, he saw that for once it was shut. The sassy artist's model never locked up to go to bed. So, she was likely out early or hadn't come home from that artist's ball, yet. He chided himself for wondering about such matters. He'd been telling himself, ever since she'd moved in, that nobody but a fool ever messed with gals where he worked or boarded. Yet he'd somehow gotten used to seeing her sprawled bare-ass on her big brass bedstead, blowing violet-scented smoke and knowing looks his way as he passed her open doorway. For, forbidden fruit or not, she sure inspired a man to wake up all the way, and he was beginning to feel the aftereffects of that beating.

He felt worse by the time he'd toted his bag to the nearby Union Depot and found himself a tall highball and a low-slung seat in the club car. They did book Pullman compartments on the coaster, but he had to change trains in less than nine hours and he knew that once he lay down, feeling this awful, he'd never get up again.

He was working on his second highball and feeling slightly more human by the time the coaster had paused at San Jose to jerk water and let passengers on and off. He felt good about San Jose. It had been good to him the time he'd spent at Stanford, taking Journalism when he wasn't punching cows or picking plums as he worked his way through college. So, when a gaggle of giggling young folk came back to the club car as the train pulled out, he assumed they were students from Stanford and that helped, some. But not enough, as they all kept jabbering and laughing like hyenas in . . . *French*? What in thunder could that many French folk, or French students, be doing aboard this train while classes were in session?

As he regarded them for some time, and they never shut up, Stringer decided they had to be the real thing. Some of the gals seemed young enough to be coeds, and a couple were real lookers. But the mostly male crowd seemed a mite long in the tooth to pass for college boys. A couple were balding and one gent was gray over the ears. They were making enough noise for a grammar school class on an unsupervised outing. That might not have bothered him as much if he hadn't been nursing a dull headache as well as a drink that didn't seem to help, or if he'd been unable to follow their lingo. He knew just enough French to try. But not enough to get all the jokes, unless he was missing something and they were just a remuda of laughing Jack and Jennie asses. He got wearily to his feet and moved out to the observation platform with his drink. There were two wicker chairs out there. Each looked as uncomfortable as the other. He sat in the one farthest from the door and watched railroad ties recede for a while, then the damned door slid open and an infernal young French gal came out to take the other seat. When she addressed him in English, albeit with a delightful accent, he decided she might not be so infernal after all. For, aside from looking like a cross between the Gibson Girl and Mimi, the upstairs maid, her striped summer-weight dress hid less of her trim figure than it was likely meant to.

He had to ask her what she'd just said, while he'd still been mad at her. She dimpled sweetly at him to reply, "I asked if we had somehow annoyed you. One could not help noticing a certain savagery in your so sudden departure, *hein*?"

Stringer smiled as sincerely as he could manage as he gallantly lied, "Not at all. I just thought you and your friends could use the extra room."

She looked relieved and said, "Mais you were there first, non? You must forgive our enthusiasm for your *tres dramatique* West. It is all so new to us. M'seur, ah . . . ?"

"MacKail," Stringer replied, removing his hat for the moment to add, "Stuart MacKail of the *San Francisco Sun*. I sign my copy as Stringer. It's a sort of inside newspaper joke."

She clapped her hands in delight and almost gushed, "I have *read* some of your features on the so-Wild West! And I catch on to the joke as well! A stringer is a, how you say, writer of the part time who prefers to be his own master, non?"

He smiled thinly and put his hat back on, saying, "Closer than most laymen get it, Miss . . . ?"

"Blanchard. Claudette Blanchard, of Pathe World News." She replied, adding, "We have been making our own feature, on film, of your so grand West. Mais, just this morning, we learned of an event we mean to capture with our cinema cameras. You have seen, perhaps, our Pathe News Cinemas?"

Stringer nodded and told her, "I sure have. We call them newsreels. The last one I saw in a 'Frisco nickel-odeon showed a French gent diving off that big tower in Paris with a pair of canvas wings strapped on. I can't say I thought much of his brain by the time he hit bottom."

She sighed and said, "Oui, tres tragique, mais a most exciting feature, non? I, Claudette, was cranking the camera when he, how you say, hit bottom? It was Pierre, inside, who moved in for the close-ups. I confess my resolve failed me when I heard the horrid sound he made in landing."

Stringer repressed a shudder as he soberly replied, "I'm glad they've yet to figure out how to make moving picture with sound and color, then. Where were the police while all this was going on? Surely someone should have told them a lunatic was about to leap to his death if Pathe News had time to find out about it."

She shrugged and explained, "We thought he might, how you say, make it? That German lunatic, Otto Lilienthal, managed to glide to a safe landing more than once before he managed to kill himself. Mais alas, his flights were never captured on film. We, and no doubt the police, were hoping for something less sad in Paris, last summer, *hein*?"

Stringer answered, dryly, "I guess *he* was, too. You say you folks are on your way to another exciting event, today, Claudette?"

She said, "Oui, a war. Nobody has ever made a moving picture of a battle in full sway before. Cameramen always seem to arrive after everyone is simply *lying* there."

Stringer smiled incredulously and asked, "Are you saying Pathe means to make a moving picture of that battle that's supposed to take place south of the border near Columbus, weather permitting?"

He learned he'd have to refrain from even mild American sarcasm when she shot him a worried look and asked what the odds on cloudy weather might be at this time of the year in Chihuahua.

He told her, "If it rained enough to matter in the Chihuahua Desert, they wouldn't have to call it a desert.

As a matter of fact we've been having a drought where it's *supposed* to rain in the west, this summer."

She looked relieved and said, "C'est bon, our film picks up nothing unless the sun is shining most brightly. One can hardly hope to capture the movement of a cavalry charge with a time exposure. There *will* no doubt be a grand cavalry charge, *non*?"

He grimaced and replied, "I wouldn't bet a week's pay on either side actually showing up. Mex guerrillas ride into battle if and when they happen to have something to ride. Calling either side cavalry could be stretching it a mite. Villa's just a bandit, or a patriot if you ask the pobrecitos who don't like the Diaz Dictatorship any more than he does. Terrazas is just a big cattle baron who's more fond of his cows than he is of cow thieves and Villa sells a heap of purloined beef north of the border, cheap. So it's more a feud than a war, or even a revolution. I don't think even Pancho Villa's ready to take on the Mex military, yet, and he's said to lead the biggest guerrilla band in Northern Mexico."

She pouted her tempting lower lip and asked him how he knew so much about an event her outfit had just heard of. He said, "I met up with Villa south of the Rio Grande a spell back, and lived to file a feature on him. That's why my reckless boss has me heading for Columbus to do a follow-up."

She stared at him adoringly and gasped, "You are on the way to cover the same story? C'est bon! You must throw up on us!"

He had to study on that before he dryly replied, "I think you have to mean throw *in* with you." And she agreed that seemed close enough.

He chuckled and told her, "I'd have to ponder that, some. I like to work alone in the field, which is why I keep turning down the better-paying staff position my paper keeps offering. No offense, but I fail to see any advantage to either side, Ma'am. I record my observations in shorthand or, more than I'd ever admit to the *San Francisco Sun*, by memory. I find I pick up my more exciting scoops by moving about, sudden. Correct me if I'm wrong. But don't you newsreel reporters have to set your cameras up and crank 'em in one place, aboard a tripod?"

She nodded but insisted, "Everyone there shall be viewing the battle from the same grandstand. Surely you were not planning to dash madly across the border to take part in it?"

He agreed that sounded like a swell way to get a nose for news shot off.

"Throw up on us, then," she said, "Your knowledge of your West and the customs of its people should prove invaluable to us. While filming a, how you say, roundup in Nevada, one of our poor cameramen got his hat shot off by a tres rude cowboy for reasons that still elude us. Had *you* been there, one feels certain the misunderstanding could have been avoided, *non*?"

He sighed and said, "I wouldn't bet a week's pay on that, either. I've never understood how the mere sight of an obvious dude inspires such uncouth target practice, either. Was your cameraman wearing a derby or straw skimmer, by any chance?"

She told him the Frenchman had in fact been cranking his fool camera with a pith helmet on. He nodded soberly and said, "There you go. If only *one* of the boys pegged a round at such a made-to-order-temptation they were going out of their way to be polite to visitors. Shiny yellow highbuttons have a similar effect on cowhands. If I *was* with your bunch I'd begin by advising one and all to dress more sensible. It's considered more dangerous than amusing to comment on the costume details of a gent dressed cow."

She nodded and insisted, "That is why you would be of so much help to us. Filming a battle should be difficult enough, without our having to cope with the so-strange customs of, forgive me, a less advanced race."

He sighed and said, "I et some fish eggs on French wafers one time. Didn't strike me as all that advanced, and you're really going to have to advance your manners a heap if you mean to get along with the folk you'll have to deal with where we're headed. The desert rats in and about Columbus ain't all that primitive. They're just mean as wolverines by nature. As for the Mex folk you'll likely meet up with as well, they *do* tend to act a mite primitive, and they're just as mean. Don't ask either breed to forgive you when you assure 'em your folk are more refined. They won't."

Then the confused worry in her big brown eyes made him relent enough to assure her with a smile, "*I* can forgive such observations because I'm more couth, and because I know it's true. But I've found it best to keep my opinions to myself whenever a gent shooting up the town ain't aiming at me in particular."

She laughed and said she'd try to remember that. Then she shot him a puzzled look and asked if he'd hold still for a personal observation. He told her to shoot and she said, "I am unable to avoid noticing that your own speech seems, how you say, cow for a well-known newspaper writer, *hein*?"

He sighed and said, "I get to go through this a heap. I was born and reared in cow country. I was orphaned young and taken in by kind relations who learned to talk English instead of the Gaelic from mighty rustic neighbors during the California Gold Rush. The kids I grew up around spoke English no better, when they weren't speaking Spanish or Miwok. I had to learn more fancy English when I decided a writer earned more money for less hardship than a cowhand. So I only talk natural when I'm talking. I hardly ever make a grammatical error when I'm typing and, when I do, my editor fixes it with his blue pencil."

She nodded soberly but told him he still sounded more like a boy of the cows than an author. He laughed and said, "It's a good thing you do your own reportage with a camera, then. You got a lot to learn about us old boys. Mark Twain talks like an English professor and writes like a farmboy. My pal, Jack London, talks like the Shanty Irish guttersnipe he was born and can hardly bear to write words of less than eight or ten letters. Do you really think Sir Walter Scott used thee and thou when he was asking his old woman what was for supper?"

She shook her head and said, "I said I understood. You are missing my meaning and, oh, I wish you spoke French. I was only trying to pay you the compliment. My point was that anyone can see how valuable your grasp of the roughness of western speech must be in dealing with the species. One doubts a reporter like you has his hat shot off tres often, *hein*?"

He grinned sheepishly and admitted, "Not as a joke. The few times I've had my hat blowed off, they were aiming at my skull."

She nodded and said, "That is why Pathe needs your assistance in assuring only Mexicans draw fire in that battle we are all marching toward, together."

"What's in it for me?" Stringer replied wearily.

She looked hurt and told and asked, "Do you imply

you would expect to be *paid* for throwing up on us, Stuart?" To which he replied, politely but flatly. "I sure can't see doing it *gratis*, to borrow one of your own words. I used to get paid a dollar a day just to herd cows and, no offense, herding Frenchmen through a crowded cowtown without losing a head sounds more complicated."

He stared back along the tracks as their train click-clacked for a while before he added, "Sounds like less fun, too. I like to work alone. Gives me a chance to meet all sorts of interesting folks I don't have to worry all that much about. I don't like to feel responsible for others, even when they know how to act in tough little towns. Sometimes it's been all I could do to get *myself* back to civilization with the story."

She looked like she was fixing to cloud up and rain tears all over him. So he said soothingly, "I'll think about it, though. We got a heap of railroad travel ahead of us before we get to Columbus. This day will be about shot by the time we get to L.A., and Lord knows how long we'll have to lay over there. That big flood in the Colorado Desert played pure confusion with rail travel inland, and right now train connections are a sometimes thing. We may well have a full night's ride ahead of us, when and if this fool coaster finally gets us to L.A. So why don't we just sleep on the notion. I may feel more like defending the honor of France after you give me time to study on it."

He saw he'd made a tactical error when she said, "C'est bon. The others will be so pleased when I tell them you are bored."

He started to tell her she had to mean on board. He decided he'd better not. The notion sounded boring as hell and he could see she was one of those stubborn gals who just refused to take no for an answer. He figured she'd call a *man* who refused to take no for an answer a brute. So he stared back along the tracks some more. Staring at her just made him feel brutal.

CHAPTER
THREE

It didn't take Stringer a whole day and a night to make up his mind. By no later than, say, 10 P.M. Claudette had sort of made his mind up for him. Before that happened she'd hauled him in to have dinner with her French pals. They'd been slumming for local color in the club car, he learned, when he wound up in the private car Pathe had up forward. Having eaten in the diners of the S.P. Line, Stringer couldn't really blame them for wanting their grub cooked French by a Chinaman who really knew his trade. The French folk treated him decently, even though few of them spoke much English and none of 'em spoke it half as well as Claudette. The commander of the expedition was an old gent with a spade beard and a Legion of Honor ribbon stuck in his lapel. The half-dozen other men dressed nigh as fancy. The four gals, including Claudette, could have dressed as nice anywhere and been accepted socially. The current Gibson Girl look was all the rage, east and west, with even old Etta Place, the Sundance Kid's pretty doxie, posing for sepia-tones with her hair pinned the same stylish way. Keeping track of the unfamiliar names of folk who couldn't say you were wrong was a bother. Stringer settled, for now, with just recalling that the old cuss in charge was called Mon Sewer LaRoche. He was

23

the one who told Stringer where to sit as they all ate buffet, which meant you got to eat with your plate in your lap. Stringer knew French folk had odd notions about eating. Aside from *what* they ate, which in this case didn't seem so odd, Frenchmen just hated to sit down to table with anyone they hadn't known long enough to trust them with the linen and silver service. It was all right to dine with most any cuss at a public cafe. You had to like 'em a mite better to feed 'em informal, like this, just as long as it was understood you didn't know 'em well enough to serve 'em at your family table, which was off limits to strangers with the possible exception of The Pope.

From the way everyone else laughed and chatted while the cook kept cooking and a shy Filipino kept piling grub on a sideboard or shoving it in people's laps, you'd never know old LaRoche was treating them like peasants. They were likely used to being treated like that by a member of the Legion of Honor. Hired help in America took a lot of shit from the boss and never let on it bothered them, come to think of it.

His dull headache seemed gone for good, now. The drinks he'd had earlier had done wonders for his battered skull, and he hadn't known how hungry he was until he'd noticed even ice cold soup tasted swell. He liked mushrooms cooked in some fancy sauce even better and once he'd enjoyed some spicy goose liver laced with little black things, he opted for a second helping and didn't ask what the black things might be. Chinese food tasted better when you didn't ask, too. He didn't see how the lumps in the goose liver could be anything ominous. They didn't have much taste of their own. It was Claudette who noticed he sure seemed to like Paddy

Something and agreed the truffles added to the enjoyment.

He almost said, "So that's what truffles are." But he never let on. He was well-read enough to know that truffles were something mighty expensive that Frenchmen got to eat. He'd never seen why fancy eaters carried on so much about caviar, either. The sour cream they served with it tasted just as good.

There was a lot to be said for just sitting around and gnawing interesting bits of this and that. The Filipino kept his wine glass filled as well and, as a Californian, Stringer knew enough about wine to tell he was getting mighty fine grape squeezings. But, as the train rolled on and the refreshments just kept coming he began to wonder when the meal was supposed to be over, and how anyone was supposed to tell. He noticed nobody else was eating or drinking as fast as he'd been. So he slowed down, feeling sort of awkward, as he realised French folk just seemed to like to talk with their faces filled. He'd been raised country, to just sit and get it over with. This bunch went right on nibbling, long after anyone back home would have pushed away from the table and gone out to hunt some strays before the sun went down completely.

Claudette had hauled him up forward to what he'd thought was to be a late dinner, or lunch as city folk had taken to calling it of late. But, as the hills outside proceeded to turn more gold than brown he revised his estimate in favor of an early supper. He wondered what they paid the kitchen help to put in such hours. More bottles were uncorked to sit on the sideboard. Californians knew wine tasted better after you let it breathe a spell. He suspected he'd already put away his fair share of that fancy French wine. It tasted so swell and went down so easy a man could abuse the privilege if he didn't watch himself. So, when he saw some of the other gents starting to puff on tailor-mades, Stringer put his plate and glass aside to get out the makings and roll one for himself. The cameraman called Pierre told everyone to regard what he was doing and Stringer knew what *droll* meant, in either lingo. He could see why some French cameramen got their hats shot off. He went on rolling. He wasn't doing anything all that dumb. Cigarettes had all been rolled by hand until some infernal frog had invented a machine to make 'em for sissies who didn't know how. He didn't think much of the smell of French tobacco, either, if one wanted to get snooty about it.

Claudette murmured something in rapid-fire French and Pierre decided to stare out the window instead of at Stringer for now.

Claudette said something else and changed places with the gent who'd been stuffing himself next to Stringer. She smiled admiringly at him and said, "You have tres clever fingers. We were not making fun of your smoking habits, Stuart. Pierre was only observing that we ought to take back a shot of an American boy of the cows rolling his own rustic cigarette, *hein?*"

Stringer said, "Bull Durham ain't rustic. It's good tobacco. If there was a tailor-made brand as smoked so honest, me and the boys would likely smoke 'em. You still have a mite to learn about us boys of cows. For one thing, you got cowboy backwards. For another thing, you got our habits a mite misread. Men who've learned to shift for themselves in the Great Outdoors get into habits that only look crude to greenhorns. Cowhands don't dress the way they do just to look funny. Every trade has its own down-to-earth costume. Working longer hours than most, cowhands get used to wearing their work duds all the time. They wear loose shirts that don't tear easy because any other kind would wind up ripped out at the shoulders by a half-way decent roper. They wear their pants tight as they can get into because loose pants can blister you unmentionable after a few days in the saddle, and a cowhand spends six twelve-hour days there, unless it's roundup time or he's driving a market herd with no days off at all. As for our funny hats, you design a better style for riding hot and cold, wet or dry, and we'll sure be proud to wear it. Cow manners may seem crude. But they're built practical, too. A man soon discovers, in a cow camp, that he has to either learn to fight good or keep his thoughts about others to himself. As for the way we eat, smoke and drink, don't buy all you read in the Wild West magazines. Cowhands may not eat *fancy*, but if you want to keep a good crew through one roundup you got to feed 'em *good*. I've seen men quit in disgust because the boss was too cheap to serve Arbuckle brand coffee. It's ground in San Francisco, expensive, because you just can't make a decent cup of coffee over an open fire unless you start out with the best brand. You want me to roll you a Bull Durham cigarette? Folk ought to try good plain tobacco before they turn up their noses at it."

She seemed to think that was a swell notion. So he gave her the first one he'd rolled, saying, "I ain't had this in my mouth yet and the fire will kill any bugs in my spit as it burns down the seam."

For some reason that seemed to strike her as mighty amusing. But, once he lit her and she'd inhaled a couple of drags as a good sport, she announced in French that, droll or not, they did grow tobacco fantastique in the *Etats Unis*. So he had to roll more samples and after the admiration had subsided, LaRoche said something to the gal and she told Stringer. "That is what I meant about you being such a treasure. You are most correct that we have much to learn about even the civilized parts of your country, and we are going into a part of it even you describe as tres savage. I can assure you poor Pierre was not trying to be rude, just now. Mais, if even an educated westerner such as yourself felt offended by his surprise at your smoking habits, consider how much trouble he could get into with Mexican bandits!"

He didn't want to get in any more trouble himself, so he made a show of glancing out at the low-hanging California sun before he said, "I said I'd study on it. Right now I'd best go on back and make sure the bag I left above a certain seat is still there and that said seat's still empty."

She shrugged and said, "By all means assure your luggage. Mais what do you need with a coach seat? We shall arrive in Los Angeles any minute, and of course this car shall be switched to the next train leaving for our final destination, non?"

He said, "That has to have traipsing through the L.A. yards beat. But sooner or later, I have to settle down for the night on one fool car or another."

She asked, demurely, "What is the matter with this one? We, of course, have sleeping compartments, forward. Why would you wish to sleep sitting up, even if, in the end, you decide not to throw up on us, *hein*?"

He had to agree that sounded tempting, and added it would save him making connections afoot, since this private car was bound for Columbus one way or another. Then he felt obliged to ask, "Are you sure there's room for me? How many sleeping compartments could even Pullman manage in one sixty-foot car?"

She said, "Allow me to think. There are ten of us and six compartments, I believe. That leaves plenty of room, since some, ah, prefer company when we retire."

Stringer reined in his curiosity just in time to avoid a full inventory of who got to sleep with whom. It was still too early for such dumb questions. He nodded and said he'd best get back with his gladstone before they reached L.A. and commenced to cut the train apart. Then he got to his feet, surprised at the way his legs felt after all that wine, and headed back to where he'd left that fool bag.

The other passengers to the rear, American or not, seemed to find his cowhand ways a mite surprising as Stringer ran both ways through the aisles, with his boot heels thunking and his spurs jingling a merry tune. They couldn't see what he was grinning about, either.

CHAPTER
FOUR

But, Rome wasn't built in a day and, as every man who wasn't born a sissy knows, to his sorrow, the torture of having to hold back when one knows it's all set, is topped only by the torture of not knowing for sure.

Claudette looked as if butter wouldn't melt in her mouth as Stringer rejoined her up forward. Everyone else went right on chawing and jawing, oblivious to both Stringer and Claudette and to the ramshackle buildings they were passing as the train rolled slower through the outskirts of a sunset red Los Angeles. Glancing down at his gladstone, the French gal told him to come with her. But when they got to a cozy compartment near the front end of the car, she just told him to put his bag on the overhead rack. When he tried to take her in his arms, she told him not to be silly. Then, as she led him back along the narrow corridor by one hand she relented enough to murmur, "I may be called upon to translate if there is any difficulty about enmeshing this car to another species of chou chou, *hein*?"

There was. After making its regular stop at the depot, the coaster was hauled out into the yards to be broken up, with some of the combination going on down to San Diego and others recoupled to go in other directions. It was Stringer, smoking on the forward platform with Claudette and Pierre, who knew the L.A. yards well enough, even in the ruby light of gloaming, to notice the yardmen seemed to be out to couple them to the mail and baggage cars meant for San Diego. He called down, "We'd better have us a dispatcher out here, boys. This car's bound for Columbus, New Mexico, on the Tucson, Douglas, El Paso line."

One of the dark figures crunching about with his derby at the level of Stringer's shins waved a clipboard back at him to reply, "I *am* the dispatcher, Cowboy. Ain't this the private car hired by Pathetic News of Paris, France?"

When Stringer assured him it was, the dispatcher held his orders up to what light remained, nodded, and announced, "South to the end of the line at Dago. That's what she reads."

Claudette gasped, "Mais non!" and might have said more if Stringer hadn't shushed her and muttered, "Let me handle it. Logic is the wrong tack to take with dumb officious types." Raising his voice to a tone of command he'd heard army shavetails get away with, he told the dispatcher, "Your orders are a mistake. Before we say anything we might wind up feeling dumb about, I work for the *San Francisco Sun* and I know Mister Huntington well enough to call him Hank to his face. These visitors to our wild and savage shores have to get to Columbus, pronto. If you cost both them and your railroad a dumb and needless delay by routing this car the wrong way, I'm going to have to tell old Hank it's a hell of a way to run a railroad, and since he just hates to have my paper call him a dumb as well as greedy octopus in print, I hope you can see who figures to get fired in hopes of calming me and these other newshawks down."

The dispatcher gulped and said, "Well, since you've explained the situation so loud and clear, I reckon we can work this out without pestering Mister Huntington. Are you with me so far?"

Dubiously Stringer told him to just keep talking as long as he didn't mention San Diego again. So the railroader laughed and said, "I got to, just a mite. Almost all the cars down these spurs are being coupled to head that way. Eastbound Pullmans and coaches are getting or have got combined a mile and a half up the other way. The occasion of all this confusion is the extra specials we got to make up for some big rodeo or something over New Mexico way. By the time I can get the cars blocking you to other spurs, the eastbound express you say you'd rather be coupled to will be long gone. We only got so many switch engines and . . ."

Stringer cut in to insist that wasn't good enough, adding, "We have to be in Columbus no later than early tomorrow morning."

The dispatcher laughed again and said, "I wish someone would leave chores to gents who know what they're doing. I was just fixing to say that Pathetic News having its own private car gives us some flexation to work with, here. You all have all the comforts built into that one car, right?"

When Stringer agreed, the dispatcher continued, "There you go. I ain't supposed to be this uppity, but lest we needlessly vex Mister Huntington, I stand ready to couple you up to a highball freight that's leaving for Texas in less'n two hours."

Stringer asked why they couldn't still shoot for the regular eastbound express if they had that much time to work with. To which the railroader replied, "The eastbound's leaving sooner. Too soon for us to move half the rolling stock in these yards for your convenience, without word one on my onion skins, here. I keep telling you I'm going *out of my way* for you all."

Stringer didn't answer. The railroader nodded and said, "There you go. Hold your fire and we'll just couple you to the rear of the highball's caboose, along with some other short run box cars they'll be dropping off along their way at jerkwaters. Highball freight moves cross country as sudden as varnish express trains because local traffic has to run up sidings outten their ways. I'd be fibbing if I said a highball could leave more than an hour after your varnish and beat it to Columbus. But, on the other hand they can still drop you off there no more than an hour or so later than you could get by that combination we just can't *get* you to afore it leaves."

Stringer agreed the railroader's suggestion made more sense than spending the whole night in the L.A. yards. So the dispatcher laughed and moved closer to scrawl cryptic chalk marks on the side of their private car. As he did so, Stringer explained to Claudette, "He's turning us into a freight car with his magic wand. That's how the brakemen on a freight train know where to drop cars off. Passenger conductors only have to call out the stops and their live freight gets off all by itself."

Claudette said the railroads of France worked much the same way. Pierre muttered something in French, Stringer knew that "Merde" meant "Shit", and then the cameraman went inside to let them worry about what was going on out here. Stringer asked what that had been about and she confided, "He observed you were acting rather, how you say, bossy for someone who did not even work for Pathe. One imagines he is jealous. You are taller than poor Pierre as well, non?"

He stared down at her uncertainly, as he just had to ask if Pierre had anything else to feel jealous about. She dimpled up at him to reply demurely, "Not if we are talking about the goings on of romantique matters. I am tres particular about whose things I might want in my compartment, or anywhere else, *hein*?"

So he tried to kiss her, and when she murmured something about the yard workers, he led her inside. But that was a tactical error. She got the lead on him, and the next thing he knew they were back with the others, and dinner was still being served. So all he could do was sit down and sip some more infernal wine, trying not to look as if he gave a damn. No man over the age of, say, fourteen ever let a gal know he was anxious if he expected to get anywhere with her. But things were sure starting to drag by the time they felt the car moving under them again. It moved for only a short time before it stopped and thudded under them now and then.

Pierre had, no doubt, done some bitching to old LaRoche, but the boss seemed to think Stringer had done them some big favor. He suspected, he said with Claudette's help, that business rivals were out to do him dirty by bribing the Southern Pacific to run them the wrong way and make them miss the fun and games in Columbus. When Claudette asked on her own if this could be true, Stringer explained, "I just hate to say anything nice about the octopus, as we fondly refer to the S.P. in California. But it's been run half-way decent since Henry Huntington took over. I'm not saying old Hank can't be bought. But buying him would cost you more than a dozen reels of battle scenes could be sold for, with color and sound thrown in, which they tell me is impossible."

Claudette translated. The old coot still looked dubious. So Stringer pointed out, "Look, the Huntingtons have the biggest mansion in Pasadena. They've got it stocked with oriental rugs big enough to play football on, as well as statuary by old Greeks and paintings by old masters. They're too coy to say what they paid for the famous Blue Boy but I can tell it was more than you'll ever get for a picture of Pancho Villa, moving or not."

He could follow her French just enough to tell she phrased that more delicately to old LaRoche, who seemed to think his motion pictures had oil paintings beat by a mile. LaRoche kept coming up with dark plots against his own immortal works until they all felt the car moving under them. When everyone but LaRoche heaved a collective sigh of relief, Stringer told them to hold the thought and got up to stride back to the rear platform. Peering up at the now starry sky he located the Dipper, saw it was out to scoop up the North Star where both of them were supposed to be, and started to duck back in to assure everyone before he decided to roll a smoke instead. He was just about out of tobacco, as well as an hour or more behind the train he should have been on, thanks to those pesky frogs inside. He'd *told* the fool gal why he preferred to work alone in the field and they were proving his point before he could even get there.

Someone must have wondered if he'd fallen off. For he wasn't half-way through with his smoke before Claudette joined him back there, to ask if anything was wrong. He shrugged and said, "We're headed east for the desert. I'd be that far already if I'd just transferred to that earlier train the way I was supposed to."

She lowered her lashes to murmur, "Oui, and without

your help we'd have no doubt been tres chagrined to discover ourselves in San Diego. I told you we'd all be better off if you threw up on us, Stuart. Have we made you so late that you cannot consider the additional comforts we have to offer some compensation for such a minor delay? The battle is not supposed to take place for at least another forty-eight hours, you know."

He shrugged and said, "Let's hope both Mex armies agree with us on the time. I'm not sure Villa knows how to tell time. I know he doesn't know how to read. The bravos riding for Terrazas have to be just as dumb, if they really mean to go through with things as planned."

He started to flick his spent smoke away, remembered you never did that in chaparral country, and crushed it underfoot instead before he took her in his arms to ask if she usually stayed up this late. She giggled and told him it wasn't nearly her usual bedtime. But, she didn't resist when he tried to kiss her this time; she kissed back and it was true what they said about French kissing. But when he braced her back against a bulkhead and tried to find out what else she had to offer, she slapped his questing hand and murmured, "Mais non! Only *clochards* make the zig zig standing up with all their clothing on, you naughty boy!"

So they just spooned for awhile on the platform, until, in the end, it was her idea to duck inside and see if the coast might be clear.

It was. Aside from the Filipino asleep in an arm chair, the main salon was deserted. Before anyone could come back for a nightcap, Stringer and Claudette were in her compartment and it didn't take him long to verify that lots of other things they said about French loving were true, unless Claudette was a mite more adventurous than other French gals. She'd obviously been anxious to wind up this way with him, as well. For, despite what she'd said about clochards, the street gypsies of Paris, she never bothered to shuck her long black stockings or lacy black corset before she had him pinned down with his bare behind to the bed covers and her long black hair unpinned to sweep his bare chest when she impaled herself on his overanxious erection. She just chuckled fondly and kept going when she felt him ejaculate almost at once. He didn't mind. He parted the curtain of soft wavy hair between them to admire the view of her bouncing breasts by the moonlight that shone through the window beside them. Her moonlit charms inspired him to greater heights, and after she was inspired to moan, "Ooh la la, I am *arriving*!" he rolled on top to make her arrive some more the old-fashioned way. But if there was one thing Claudette was not, it was an old-fashioned girl. For, when they finally had to stop and see if they could catch their second wind, she proceeded to strip down all the way and demand, not suggest, that they cut out this kid stuff and get down to some serious sex.

CHAPTER
FIVE

Not even Stringer could last a whole night making love to Claudette, bless her back-breaking gymnastics, so they were both asleep in each other's naked arms when a beam of desert sunlight shot through the grimy glass above them to jolt them into wakefulness. As Stringer muttered, "What the hell . . . ?" the French girl murmured, "We are not moving. Mon Dieu, draw the shades before some species of rude railroad worker peeks in at us!"

Stringer told her to hold the thought as he propped himself up on one elbow for a thoughtful stare outside, saying, "This window shouldn't be facing any sunrise if we're aimed *east*. So where could we be aimed?"

He stared soberly out at miles and miles of knee-high greasewood, adding, "This has to be the Colorado Desert. There ain't another desert half as tedious. So how come? At the rate we were moving we should have been in cactus country by now, only we ain't. We can't even be on the far side of the Colorado River, and we should have crossed it no more than four or five hours out of L.A., even by freight train."

Claudette sat up, her pert nipples peeking through her long hair at the same scenery as she marveled, "The sage flats of Nevada may have looked so monotonous, coming the other way, mais wherever we may be, it can't be New Mexico, *hein*?"

He told her he'd just said that as he swung his bare feet to the deck and proceeded to grope his way into his clothes. It took him a while to find one sock, which was under Claudette's striped dress. They'd both undressed the night before in a hurry, in pitch blackness. When he rose in his boots, jeans and shirt to get down his gladstone and open it near her knees, she asked him why he seemed to be going for his gun. He strapped the gun rig around his hips as he told her, "I ain't sure, yet. If there's a town on the far side of this car it could be a tough one. If there ain't, we could be in even bigger trouble."

He saw they were in bigger trouble as soon as he strode to the forward platform and stepped out on it. There wasn't anything on either side but miles of empty landscape. Their one car stood alone like a dead cigar butt in the middle of a vast wool blanket of greasewood gray. It wasn't even an interesting shade of gray. The Colorado Desert was like that. The single track spur they were on ran north, not east, toward a distant clump of dark objects already heat-shimmered by the morning sun. He got down and circled south to see the tracks that way just drew together at the vanishing point near the horizon. As he stood there cussing, some of the others came out on the rear platform to stare about in wonder. Old LaRoche demanded to know where they were. Stringer was doing his best to explain when Claudette came out, fully dressed and demure as ever, to translate. So he told her, "We've been sidetracked, literally. Sometime during the night they stopped that freight, backed it up this spur, and uncoupled us. I'm still working on the reason."

Once LaRoche had it straight in his head, he opined he and he alone had been sabotaged by the Edison Film Trust, if not the Communards who hated him for being an aristocrat despite his fervid loyalty to La Republique. Stringer told Claudette, "I have to allow someone surely done us dirt, for whatever reason. We have to be miles off the main line. They build these spurs to serve mining camps, sawmills and such. I can't see a *sawmill* out here amid the murmuring greasewoods. But there's some buildings to the north, a lot closer than we are to anywhere else. So, I reckon I'll just mosey up there."

When Claudette explained this to her companions, an older cameraman objected that the tracks on which they were stranded could hardly be out of service if said town was still in use. Stringer nodded but explained, "Ghost towns are sometimes haunted by old-timers left behind when the company as built 'em pulls out. I might be able to at least find out where in thunder we *are*. At worst, there ought to be water wells up yonder and, sooner or later, we're going to run out of it. No matter how much you folk think you have in this car's water tanks, go easy on it 'til I get back. I figure an hour or less each way."

Then he got his hat and jacket and started up the spur as everyone waved to him from the shade of the front platform. They were no fools. It was already getting hot enough to sizzle spit on the sun-baked cross ties. But he didn't spit. That was dumb in desert country. He'd only been guessing when he said there could be water up ahead. Sometimes, when an outfit pulled out, they pulled up the tube wells while they were at it.

It was a long, dull trudge. Even the bugs were hiding in the meagre shade offered by the slate gray greasewood. The center of this dull desert was as quiet and

about as flat as the carpet in a funeral home. It seemed
to be taking forever, but it was more like the better part
of an hour before he made it to the few sun-silvered
buildings still standing and wondered why he'd bothered.

Foundation blocks left scattered among the encroach-
ing gray brush hinted at a once-sizeable operation. The
dirty white film of crude borax in the storage shed near
the end of the rails told him why anyone had ever
wanted to build anything here to begin with. Desert
borax wasn't mined. It was scraped from the dry mud
bottoms of long extinct lakes. He didn't really care just
where such a *playa* might have been, around here, before they'd scraped away the top few inches of root-kill-
ing salts and given it all back to the greasewood. He
found a water pump behind the husk of a dead saloon. It
seemed to be in working order. A black widow spider
dripped out of the spout on a silvery thread as he tried to
work the valves. From the way the handle pumped up
and down, he suspected it only needed to have its
leather flap valves primed with water. They could likely
use wine if all else failed. Using water for anything that
experimental could be fatal, if this or some other pump
around here couldn't be made to work. A smaller shed
across the way had also been left standing. He headed
for it, then whipped out his .38 S&W as the door of the
shed creaked on its hinges. He called out a couple of
times, got no answer, and fired a round through the dry
planking to see what would happen.

Nothing did. Another vagrant desert breeze swung
the door the other way. He decided that had to be what
was haunting the shed. He still moved in fast and low.
But once he'd kicked the door open and found the place
deserted, he muttered to the cobwebs all around, "So

I'm acting proddy? I got a right to be and what have you spiders been up to in here, all this time?"

That was easy enough to see. The only furnishings consisted of a built-in bench, with some shelves above it. A telegraph key was screwed to the work bench. Like the pump across the way, it seemed to be in working order. There was nothing to it but a flexible spring that made or broke contact between two electrodes and the wires connected up about right. After that, it got more tedious. Like the leather valves of the pump across the way, the acid in the battery jars above the key had long since evaporated in the mummy's breath of the desert. He stepped back outside to see if that was even worth thinking about. It was. Wires ran up from the shed to a single-line strung across the desert in the general direction of the main line. It looked intact as far as he could follow it against the cobalt sky. He nodded and began to reach for his makings as he muttered, "Right, it was a gut-and-git borax operation. They left stuff behind that could be bought again cheaper than it could be taken out. If they never bothered with this end of their telegraph line, the other end ought to be in as good condition. Now all we have to do is tote some liquid refreshment up here from that infernal car."

It took as long getting back to the stranded Pathe party as it had to reach the abandoned mining operation, and once he did, nobody wanted to help him. They'd been at the wine again and Claudette's explanation of his words seemed to lose something in the translation. LaRoche seemed to feel he was too important to ever die and insisted that if anyone was out to murder them outright they'd all have been murdered in their sleep the night before. Stringer swore and insisted, "I don't know *what* they were out to do to us, because I don't know who *done* it. But I do know this desert figures to murder us *for* them, unless they send help and, somehow, I don't trust such sneaky bastards enough to leave our lives in their hands. So I reckon I'll just have to save all you dumb frogs before you waste all the damned water!"

He went into the kitchen and told the two-man crew there what he wanted. They either didn't follow his drift or didn't want to. He still helped himself to a potato sack by spilling the contents around the feet of the wailing Chinaman and patted the grips of his .38 at the Filipino when the latter reached for a cleaver as he was stuffing the sack with bottles. They both went out to tell on him. Stringer hefted the sack after he'd filled it with bottles of wine, fancy French vinegar, and some bottled water. It was heavy, but he knew he might need more. Claudette came in to ask him what he'd done to make the Filipino cry. He explained he had better use for the stuff where he was going and that he'd pack more if only he could. She said, "C'est bon, allow me to help, then."

He almost said no before he nodded grudgingly and said, "Right. I don't see why they'd need a translator with me way off in that ghost town." Then he filled a lighter flour sack for her and told her to get her shady hat. She did so, as they carried their booty up the corridor, and he helped her down from the front platform. As they started up the tracks, LaRoche came out to demand some explanation. Stringer said, "Screw him. We've already told him, and he says it won't work."

Claudette dimpled and replied, "Mais non, I would rather screw *you* some more. You said there is some shade at that most ghostly town ahead?"

He laughed and told her to just keep walking, explaining, "There's not enough left to qualify as a ghost town. I might want to give you a big old kiss if this works."

"And should it not work, Stuart?" She asked. To which he could only answer, "I may as well kiss you anyway, before our spit dries up totally. Don't look so morose, little darling. It takes a good two days to die of thirst out here, and we've still got water enough for at least three."

She sighed and said, "Alas, by the time we all perish, that Mexican war will be over, non?"

He sighed back and said, "Non. At the rate they're going at it, they'll likely still be slaughtering one another after we've both died of old age. I'd rather go *that* way than any other I can think of. So let's hope my high school science teacher knew what he was talking about."

Back in high school, Stringer had been a lot more interested in Miss Beverly Breen who'd sat across from him than the droning of poor old Mister Smiley's lectures on general science, which only went to show how dumb most boys are in high school. For he'd never gotten anywhere with Miss Beverly Breen, while a lot of things Mister Smiley had droned at him had come in handy from time to time. Getting to the deserted borax works was a lot less tedious, this time, even though the sun was even hotter and the stuff they were packing got heavier with every step. When they finally got there, Claudette sunk wearily to the back steps of the abandoned saloon, but watched with interest as Stringer primed the pump with wine. She said the species of rusty machinery could hardly deserve the vintage of '93 but he told her, "Water of any vintage is worth more out here. In dry country, liquor is for fun and water is for fighting over."

He let the dry leather soak up more wine to make sure it was wet through before he risked cracking only half-soft leather as he reached again for his makings, remembered again that he was out of tobacco, and asked if she'd brought along any tailor-mades. She said she hadn't. Stringer sighed and said, "Oh, well, I was trying to cut down. Let's hope I don't have to cut out all my bad habits, like *drinking*, at once."

He primed the pump again with the last of the bottle, screwed the cap back on, and gingerly started pumping. The valves felt right, but nothing much seemed to be happening and Claudette was saying rude things about American plumbing, when all of a sudden, a clot of spider webbing and dead bugs shot out ahead of a flood of stinking inky-black water. She gasped, *"Merde alors!* Do you expect us to drink that filth?" So he just kept pumping and, sure enough, crud gave way to mud and then the pump was watering the dust with clear cool water. He wet his Stetson under the spout and put it back on, letting go of the pump handle as he said, "So far so good. Now all we have to worry about is *starving* to death. Let's see what we can do in that telegraph shack."

She tagged along with her own bottles, like a sport, but as she stood in the doorway watching him pour vinegar into the dry battery jars, she repeated the opinion of her associates that his droll notion was not *practique*. He took her sack from her to get at more vinegar as he growled, "Mister Smiley said adding acetic acid to sulfuric made it stronger. Lord knows, the acid in these jars lost its *water* long ago. But the dry crud left is still supposed to be acid and that's what we need right now. You see these metal plates I had to haul out to replace the liquid? Well, half of 'em are zinc and the others are copper. I forget just how Mister Smiley said it works. I do know he said that when you hang zinc and copper in acid it sets up an electric current between the wires connected to 'em. This battery of jars looks old-timey, which is why they may have been left behind. But you only need a weak current to work a telegraph set, and that's likely just as well. I don't see how we'll manage a *strong* one."

But manage they did and, Stringer was as surprised as Claudette when the set on the table commenced to buzz at them like a brass sidewinder. He flipped the receiving mode off and muttered, "That sounded like railroad sending. Nobody's trying to talk to us, yet. The last gent who used this set just left it open to the line when he wandered away. Let's see if I can get somebody's attention."

He could, albeit it took a long time for someone to notice the halting signal corps code he was sending, and wire back for him to cut the comedy and get off the line. Stringer just kept sending S.O.S. until someone at the other end relented and asked him who might be in trouble and where.

After that, it was easy. The Southern Pacific Railroad had no idea why someone had deposited paying passengers in the middle of the Colorado Desert, agreed it seemed a hell of a way to run a railroad, and said that help would soon be on the way.

When Stringer explained this to Claudette it was she who kissed him and, once he had her pinned against the inside wall of the shed, confided that she'd always wondered what it might feel like to do la zig zig like the naughty *clochard* girls under the bridges of Paris.

So they found out, and it wasn't half bad. But they both agreed it was better in bed and that they'd best stop, after this one more time, lest Pathe News leave without them.

CHAPTER
SIX

There was another argument when a lone locomotive finally showed up late that morning. The engine crew agreed it sure seemed odd to find a private car up a spur that hadn't been used for a coon's age. But they wanted to haul the Pathe car back to the L.A. yards until Stringer asked them how well they knew the brakeman of that overnight highball. When they both confessed they hardly knew the cuss at all, Stringer said, "That's good. For I know the one and original Henry Huntington better, and I doubt that brakeman will be working for him anymore. I still have to think about a certain dispatcher. It works either way."

When the engineer growled that he wasn't about to help anyone get a fellow member of the Railroad Brotherhood in trouble Stringer told him, pleasantly enough, "He got himself in trouble. Before you boys even consider anything dumb, I'd best warn you I've already been on the wire to your company headquarters and that you're hauling us at least to Tucson and hitching us up to another eastbound with no ifs ands or buts!"

The fireman protested, "We ain't authorized to move off our own section!" To which Stringer replied, curtly, "I just said not to if, and or but me. You'll do as I say, or I'll see nobody who reads the *San Francisco Sun* will ever hire either of you again. I know I don't know your names, yet. Would you like to bet I can't find out? There has to be *someone* working for this line who isn't in on some sort of plot to keep cash-paying passengers from getting to where they paid to go. On time."

They both assured him he had them all wrong, as they had never heard word one about any such intentions.

He nodded curtly and said, "I'll buy that when and if you get this car where it's supposed to be by now. If there's any more of this bullshit, you can commend your souls to Jesus because your asses will belong to me!"

And so, Stringer and his French friends found themselves parked on a more sensible siding of the modest Columbus yards, albeit well after sunset. Since all the noise was coming from the usually sleepy little cowtown, it was safe to assume nobody had gotten around to a battle yet, in the brooding darkness to the south.

How friendly he still felt towards any infernal frog, with the possible exception of Claudette, was up for grabs. They'd made him late as hell and damned near gotten him killed. His only consolation was that had he not been along, even pretty Claudette could have wound up dead. They obviously needed someone who knew the territory better to watch over them. But where in the U.S. Constitution did it say it was *his* duty? He didn't work for Pathe and, at the rate things were going, never wanted to. But he never let on as he kissed Claudette adios on the rear platform and just told her he meant to scout the town a mite. Covering past events like these had taught him that finding a hotel room or even a pool table to lie down on after your legs gave out could be an expensive if not impossible proposition. So, there was just no telling how he might feel about old Claudette, and that cozy sleeping compartment, once he'd stretched his legs a mite.

It didn't take much leg stretching to get from one end of the town to the other. But everything in between called for a wary eye as drunks staggered out, or got thrown out, of the spanking new saloons that had been feed stores, hat shops and such a few days back. Under normal conditions there just weren't enough folk in Columbus or working on the outlying spreads to justify more than one saloon, even if they served Indians. There were likely more Indians about, than anyone else during normal times. Stringer hadn't made his mind up about the Luna Indians. They were said to be Christians assimilated to Spanish culture, and so no better or worse than Mexicans in the eyes of most local Anglos. Stringer knew how he felt about the Apaches to the north or the Yaqui to the south. Everyone felt much the same about Apaches, and Yaquis scared hell out of *that* truculent breed. The Apaches had been acting sensible for the last few summers and the Yaquis hardly ever left their home range in the Sierra Madres, so what the hell. He doubted even one of those two Mex armies would show up.

A lot of other folk must have. As he strode the streets of Columbus, Stringer saw more dudes than you could shake a stick at.

He now felt better about those French dudes back on the siding. Men sporting derbies and high button shoes had the cowfolk of Columbus clearly outnumbered ten or more to one, even though the way some obvious cowhands wore *their* hats indicated the big show had drawn good old boys from near and far. You could generally tell a rider's home range from the way he crushed the crown of his hat. Hardly anyone but Texans favored high crowned ten gallons creased down the front, while Arizona riders copied their own Arizona Rangers by having four dimples and a flat brim, Canadian Mounty style. Riders from north of Santa Fe wore their hats telescoped in the Colorado Crush that made them look Spanish from any distance. The many army men he passed had their cavalry hats creased on top and dimpled on either side, just as Stringer wore his own old army hat. Some of the troopers were colored. That meant the old Tenth Cav was in town. That, in turn, made Stringer suspect he'd been sent on a snipe hunt. Staging a battle smack on the border under the watchful eye of at least two cavalry regiments, white and black, made no sense at all.

To confirm his suspicions, Stringer paused to admire a black staff sergeant watering his bay at a public trough. His first try for a howdy was met with wary silence. White strangers dressed cow and wearing a six-gun could have that effect on colored troopers. He got a slight smile out of the cuss when he asked if he had the honor of addressing a member of the Buffalo Soldier Regiment. The sergeant nodded soberly and replied, "That's what Mister Lo called us when we was whupping his Comanche ass, Sir."

Stringer nodded knowingly and said, "I met up with the Tenth Cav down Cuba way one time. It was atop San Juan Hill. I came up along with Colonel Roosevelt and the other white boys who sort of followed your outfit up the slope."

The burly sergeant suddenly grinned widely and decided, "You was there, if that's how you remembers it. Most folk seem to think you Rough Riders took that hill whilst us shines tagged along to tidy up after your chargers, which would have been a chore, since everyone charged up that hill on foot, at a slow walk indeed. Wasn't that smokeless powder the Spanish used a bitch?"

Stringer nodded and said, "I didn't like their British shrapnel, either. I wasn't with the Rough Riders, exactly. I was covering the fighting for my newspaper. I'm called Stringer MacKail, by the way."

The sergeant turned out to be Calvin Green. Stringer asked what the Tenth was doing in these parts, the Luna being so sedate, and Green went wary again as he answered, "We just go where they sends us." Then he suddenly brightened and asked, "Say, might you be the same MacKail who put it in the papers that it *was* us, the colored troops, as really took San Juan Hill that time?"

Stringer shrugged modestly and said, "I had to. A good newspaper man is supposed to call things as he sees 'em, not as they read better. Colonel Roosevelt wasn't the one who screwed you boys out of the glory. He told me so when we met up in the Yellowstone park a while back. Another reporter called Richard Harding Davis filed that story about the Rough Riders charging up San Juan Hill without asking anyone who'd been there. He was the same cuss who allowed it had been a splendid little war."

The black sergeant looked disgusted and said, "He must not have seen much of it, then. There's no such thing as a splendid war and I reckon all wars seem just as big to the men who die in 'em. What are you doing here in Columbus, Mister MacKail?"

Stringer said, "The same as you, I suspicion. We don't have to talk about Pancho Villa if you have orders not to."

But Green just grinned and said, "Shoot, that was

before I knew who you was. We just have units from four or five regiments here, making up about a brigade in all, if them Mex boys gets foolish about the border. My officer talks to me just as natural as you do, Mister MacKail, and he says nothing's fixing to happen. Neither Mex side has any military training. But nobody who can tell his ass from his elbow would ever tell the other side just where to meet him and then tell him what *time*! Our looie says that if one fool Mex shows up it'll just be a made up show for the tourists, like a bullfight, see?"

Stringer shrugged and said, "I've seen some mighty messy bullfights. Nobody but the bull is supposed to get killed, as a rule, but some old boys do get fired up once they know the gals are watching and that they'll get extra points for acting sort of stupid. Do you mind my asking just what your orders *are*, should things get out of hand, Sergeant?"

Green shook his head and said, "Our orders are simple. As long as they keeps whatever they think they're up to outside the borders of These United States, we ain't supposed to do nothing. But if one Mex, or one Mex bullet invades the peace and tranquility of *our* country, we gets to mow the sons of bitches down. We got us a mess of them new Maxim machine guns. They'll be set up to cover the fool grandstand and all the fools sitting in 'em. I wish we'd had guns like that when I was fighting Mister Lo in my younger days. Ain't no uppity Mex gonna invade this country with Mister Maxim telling him he can't!"

Stringer agreed even Mex federales, or regular army, would be unlikely to try that in defiance of U.S. troops armed with automatic weapons. So they shook on it and he moved on.

Stringer knew there'd be more local gossip in any one of the saloons. But for now he decided to just get the feel of the place in case he ever wanted to leave it in a hurry.

Stringer's next encounter was less friendly. A few doors up, he noticed the dimly illuminated sign of an all-night Western Union office. He'd never understood why that particular company seemed out to hide its offices behind such discreet, dull yellow and locomotive black signs. Everyone else agreed it paid to advertise. The dentist across the street was easier to find, having hung out a big gold tooth. But, having found the infernal telegraph office, through no effort on their part, Stringer was reminded that he'd arrived over a day late and that even if he didn't have anything to report, yet, Sam Barca often wired him instructions on those occasions when Sam knew where the hell he was. Neither of them bothered with the Bell System's newfangled long distance telephone lines unless they just had to. Bell Telephone did advertise, a lot, but so far they had a heap of wires to string before they'd ever make good on that mighty wild promise to have every housewife in the country swapping cake recipes and gossip on one big party line. Western Union left you with a written record as well, and Sam fussed when it cost a nickel a word.

Stringer didn't notice his route to the glass door of the telegraph office was being blocked by a burly gent wearing an undertaker's dark suit and a brace of cross-draw Colt .45s until he tried to politely step around the stranger, only to be rudely blocked and told, "You don't want to send no wires, MacKail."

Stringer stared back just as hard, smiled just as unfriendly, and said, "Sure I do. Since you seem to know my name, you seem to have the advantage on me, amigo."

The stranger replied, "Sure I have the advantage on you. I make it at least one extra gun and considerable experience in matters involving such weaponry. You don't want to know my name. You already know more than a boy your size ought to mess with. They tell me there's a westbound train coming through just after midnight. You can board it on your own two feet, or catch yourself a later one, in a box. So what's your pleasure, pencil pusher?"

Stringer considered the options offered before he chuckled fondly and said, "It won't work. I've had some experience as well. When a sober man's words make no sense I have learned to consider what he's trying to get me to do."

The gunslick scowled harder and replied, "There's no mystery as to what I want you to do, MacKail. I want you to get out of town or, if that don't tickle your fancy, feel free to go for your gun any time you like."

Stringer shook his head and said, "You really must have me down as a city boy. Nobody would send a newspaper man back to his pressroom with a secret they didn't want to read in banner headlines, even if he had one. I've no idea what I'm supposed to have on your present employers, but anyone can see they sent you to shut me up, permanently. You likely have one of those mail order private licenses, but you don't want to gun anyone in cold blood in the middle of even a small incorporated township with its own law. So you're trying to get me to draw first, or try to. You must think you're pretty good, cocksucker."

The hired gun gasped and it almost worked. Then he laughed in a surprisingly boyish way and replied,

"*You've* been around a mite as well, I see. Did you really think you could get that .38 out ahead of me? It ain't even tied down, and you're so right about me being good."

Stringer shrugged and replied, "At the rate we're going, we'll just never know, will we? I'm here to cover that Mexican hoedown, not to be interviewed by a coroner's jury. I fear your chosen profession is about to go the way of the beaver trade, you poor cuss. This is a brand new century and the days when one gent could gun another and just swagger off are about over. Have you considered making buggy whips for fun and profit? You're just going to get yourself shot by another asshole or hung by the law at the rate you're going."

The older gunslick looked hurt and replied in an injured tone, "There will always be a demand for my sort of services as long as fresh-mouthed pests like you draw breath, and let it out so indiscreet. Might I persuade you to slap leather if I was to say something mean about your mother or your manhood?"

Stringer asked, "Do I look like a Mex matador? I ain't worried about a cocksucker's opinion of my manhood, since he'd hardly be in a position to know. If you'd like to call me a son of a bitch I'd be proud to accompany you to Fist City, though."

The burlier but now bewildered professional bully protested, "Hold on, I'm a hired gun, not a damned old prize fighter. You must be as loco as they say. Whoever heard of challenging a dangerous cuss like me to a fist fight?"

Stringer shrugged again and said, "Well, I won't make you meet me after school if you're too sissy. I was only offering to settle this argument in a way the Columbus law might overlook. With this many drunks in town tonight, I doubt they have a tank big enough to hold everyone who throws less than fatal punches before the night is over, do you?"

The gunslick growled, "I wasn't told to treat you less than fatal. I'm counting to ten. Then I'm going to go for my guns. You can do whatever you've a mind to."

Stringer stood there as his tormentor slowly got to nine and added, "No shit, now . . . ten!"

Then Stringer observed, "If you want to take your boots off I'd sure like to see if you can count to twenty."

The gunslick roared, "You mule-headed young son of a bitch!" So Stringer hit him, hard, with the vicious left hook. Then he threw his right to further ruin the bigger man's bridgework and send him crashing back through the glass door of the Western Union office.

The shattered glass didn't do the gunslinger much good, either, as he wound up with his knees draped over the wooden bottom of the door with the rest of him inside, knocked galley west on the floor tiles with considerable amounts of his blood mixing with the shiny shards of broken glass all over the place. Stringer ducked through the remains of the door and hunkered down to empty the gent's two holsters as well as a vest pocket stuffed with a .32 whore pistol. Meanwhile, a crowd had gathered out front, and the Western Union clerk behind the counter was calling hellfire and damnation down on both their heads.

Stringer got back to his feet and ambled over to the counter, saying, "Buenos noches. I'd be Stringer MacKail if you have any wires for me, yet."

The clerk protested, "Are you out of your mind? You just now busted twenty dollars worth of glass and littered our fresh-mopped floor with the mangled results! I'm going to have the law on you, cowboy!"

Stringer replied in the same calm tone, "Simmer down. I'm not a cowboy and the law ought to be here any minute. Meanwhile, do you have any messages for me or not?"

The clerk insisted he'd never heard of anyone called MacKail until someone by that name had shoved another drunk through his doorglass. So Stringer reached for a pad of yellow telegram forms on the counter between them and said, "I'd best let my home office know where I am, while I still can. Do you have a pencil handy?"

When the outraged clerk suggested they might have one at the lunatic asylum he'd escaped from, Stringer rummaged about in his denim jacket, got out his own pencil stub, and proceeded to fill in Sam Barca on his recent misadventures, muttering, "I got to pick up some tobacco while I'm about it. I hope you and the saloons ain't all that's open at this hour."

He'd just finished his terse message when a skinny old gent with a tin star pinned to his vest ducked through the shattered door, nudged the unconscious man on the floor with a boottip for signs of life and, being rewarded by a groan, came over to the counter to nod at both of them and say, "Evening. I don't suppose either of you gents would like to tell me how that other poor cuss wound up in such obvious distress?"

As the clerk pointed at him, Stringer slid the three guns he'd helped himself to along the counter toward the lawman, saying, "I cannot tell a lie, Marshal. I hit him twice, with my fists. He was wearing this artillery at the time and he called me a son of a bitch."

The old timer glanced soberly down at the six-gun Stringer was wearing, nodded, and opined, "I have seen such remarks turn out more fatal." Then he turned to the clerk to mildly ask, "Did you hear the passing of such a remark, Hiram?" To which the clerk flatly replied, "The first I knew, the one on the floor came flying in here, backwards, glass and all. This one says his name's MacKail, Marshal."

The older man turned back to Stringer, his bony right hand resting casually on the grips of his own side-draw Peacemaker, as he mildly observed, "You really ought to have at least one witness at times like these, and I'd sort of like to see some personal identification, Mister MacKail."

Stringer carefully got out his billfold, making no sudden moves as he opened it and handed it over. The old man took it with his left hand, leaving his gun hand right where it was, as he scanned Stringer's press pass, California gun permit, and other papers. As he handed it back with a curt nod he said, "I've read your stuff. Our Columbus paper buys its outside news from your syndicate. Now what can you tell me about the other disturber of the peace, old son?"

Stringer said, "He allowed to being a hired gun. He tried to get me to draw first. I thought it made more sense to just hit him a few good licks."

The marshal nodded soberly and said, "You thought right. We don't hold with homicide in this town and I've always been of the opinion that a man who picks fights for money is lower than a sheep herder. Do you know why he was out to cause you harm or injury, Mister MacKail?"

Stringer answered, truthfully, "You'll have to ask him when he wakes up. I'll be switched with snakes if I can think of a sensible reason to have me put out of business so rudely. I'm only here to cover that brawl between Villa and Terrazas. I can't be the only newspaper man in town, and if someone was out to keep it a secret I don't see what good gunning just me would do. I only mean to fill one seat in the stands when and if the battle comes off."

The old lawman sighed and said, "It ain't no secret. They've put up posters. Let's see who the jasper might be."

Stringer stayed put, leaning against the counter, as the town law moved over to the unconscious form on the floor, hunkered down to go through the gent's duds, and when the gunslick asked what happened and where he was, the older man muttered, "Go back to sleep. You ought to be ashamed of yourself, letting another man knock you on your ass whilst you was packing three guns."

The marshal found a wallet, pulled out a voter registration card, and muttered, "I wish they didn't hand these out to just any cuss who asks for one. I sort of doubt anyone named Walker votes all that regular in Flagstaff, Arizona Territory, but we got the alias on file and such handy cards are almost the trademark of an owlhoot who don't like to get picked up for vagrancy."

Stringer asked, "Don't most hired guns like to pack a private detective's permit, Marshal?" To which the old timer replied with a nod, "They do. But not even a Nevada judge is apt to issue one to a wanted outlaw. It appears to me you just decked a gent who goes by the name of Walker because he's wanted for more than one stickup under the name of Jones. It usually works the other way around, but it stands to reason *some* folk have to start out Jones. Unless my memory's starting to go, there's some bounty money on this cuss, Mister Mac-Kail."

Stringer said, "You can call me Stringer, the way the

rest of my friends do, seeing it was you who saved me from the brute, if you follow my drift, Marshal."

The old timer did. He grinned up at Stringer to reply. "Well, Lord knows, my old woman and me could use the money. Are you sure you don't want in, ah, Stringer?"

The newspaper man shrugged and said, "Not if it means I have to bother with depositions and hanging around for the trial. If he's already wanted, you don't need me as a witness to an altercation that was no more than a street brawl, do you?"

The telegraph clerk protested, "Hold on. Who gets to pay for all that busted glass if we're talking about just letting it go as an unpunished scuffle?"

The marshal got back up, saying, "The town will buy you a new front door if you'll just behave yourself. If you don't, it won't. As for punishment, this jasper on the floor only gets to hang once. But that ought to be enough, even if he did bust your door in attempting to escape, as anyone can plainly see."

Then the old-timer turned to Stringer to say, "You'd best just finish your business here and be on your way, old son, seeing you took no important part in my arrest, as I recall."

So Stringer told the clerk to send his wire to the *San Francisco Sun*, night rates, collect, and then they all shook on it and parted friendly.

Outside, a curious cuss with his hat crushed Colorado asked Stringer what was going on in there. Stringer shrugged and said, "Marshal's got a wanted outlaw under arrest, or he will have, once the rascal wakes up."

Another nighttime rubbernecker laughed and said, "Old Windy can sure get testy when they refuses to come quiet. They call him Windy because he likes to go on about the old days when the Murphys and McSweens were shooting it out up in Lincoln County. Says he rode with Pat Garrett when the law had had enough of the murderous rascals. That might or might not be so. But, you got to hand it to old Windy when it comes to keeping things peaceable down this way. I seen him nail a Luna horse thief on the run at a hundred and fifty yards one time. You're a stranger in these parts, ain't you, young feller?"

To which Stringer could only reply, "Sort of. It seems *someone* in these parts knows me better than I know him. Or maybe them."

CHAPTER
SEVEN

Columbus was tiny by small town standards and went to bed with the chickens as a rule. But thanks to the unruly strangers who'd flocked in from far and wide to view the impending gun battle, the one main street was still running wide open as midnight approached. So Stringer stepped around a wooden Indian to pick up some tobacco when he saw the chance. The pretty young gal behind the counter was proud to sell him a half-dozen small bags of Bull Durham at only twice what they'd have cost him in San Francisco, and told him the cigarette papers came separate and cost extra in New Mexico Territory. He doubted that they'd treat him so mean in Santa Fe. But he'd covered the Alaska Gold Rush, so he didn't argue. When she told him she had front row tickets to the battle, at only five dollars apiece, he did feel obliged to remark that he'd heard the promoters of the event were charging a buck a shot. She shrugged and replied that she just worked there. He said he had a press pass. She didn't argue. She didn't know what a press pass was, she said, since her usual occupation was chambermaiding at the one hotel near the railroad stop. When he asked what were the odds on hiring a room at said hotel, she just laughed, sort of dirty, and allowed he could use the bedroll she'd spread on the flat roof above them for two bits an hour until she needed it her- self, later.

It wasn't too clear whether she meant he'd have to get up when she closed up shop, or whether he'd wind up paying extra by the hour. She wasn't bad-looking. But he figured even if he was willing to pay for such pleasures, he could hardly afford to pay for the carnal company of a gal who considered her bedroll worth so much money *empty*. So he paid for the tobacco and papers before she could charge him extra for her smile, and ducked out to roll the first decent smoke he'd had for hours.

As he rolled one in the deep shadows of the overhang out front, he morosely regarded the passing crowd, aware that anyone who'd sent one gunslick after him could just as easily have sent two. The folk moving up and down the street on foot, on ponies, and even aboard some horseless carriages, seemed more lost and restless than bent on bodily harm. He suspected that they, like him, were mostly looking for a more sensible way to kill time than Columbus had to offer at prices anyone could afford. He knew what he was doing in town. By now, some of the others should have had second thoughts. There was less than a fifty-fifty chance that anything was going to happen, and while New Mexico was mighty hot in the daytime, its nights got downright *cold*. Stringer had been raised on high and dry semiarid rangeland. So he'd learned to ignore goosebumps under his denim jacket after dark. But these parts stood over three thousand feet above sea level, and he knew the dry, thin air would be frosting his pumpkins by the time the sun came up to fry them all some more. Unlike the mixed crowd of Anglos, Mexicans, Indians and colored troopers, he *did* have a warm and cozy place to bunk, in fact, if Claudette would only let him keep the covers over them for a change. But as he lit his smoke he decided to study on that a bit. Someone was gunning for him. It hardly seemed fair to expose Claudette to danger, no matter how much she liked to expose herself. He had no call to get anyone else with the Pathe crew killed in the cross fire, either. They'd been a bother to him through no fault of their own, and they'd tried to treat him decent, even if they had used up all his Bull Durham and almost made him miss the show.

He knew that by now the hired gun he'd clobbered ought to be awake, and even willing to chat. Men locked up had nothing better to do. But the trouble with asking a hired gun who'd sent him was that even when they seemed willing to tell you, they tended to lie. He had nothing to offer a man being held for more serious misdeeds in other parts. Jones had no reason to deal from the top of the deck with the man who'd handed him over to the law. He was more likely to try and get someone else in trouble with a tall tale involving, say, William Randolph Hearst or some local big shot who'd be vexed as hell to be accused of attempted murder by a total stranger. Stringer could only hope that his luck might hold until he figured it out for himself.

A carload of Mexicans wearing gringo Stetsons drove by. The breeze of their passing sent a shiver up Stringer's thinly-clad spine. They were in a Maxwell touring car that came with a canvas top, only they'd apparently lost it as they aimlessly toured the tiny town, disturbing such peace as there was with the choke set to make them sound as if they were running on Chinese firecrackers instead of naphtha. Stringer had read that most such engines now ran on gasoline, a sort of glorified lamp oil less explosive than naphtha. But there was no mistaking that dry cleaner's stink in the white smoke they were trailing up and down the street. If they weren't careful, some drunken cowhand was sure to answer in kind. Those brass head lamps made a tempting moving target.

But nobody was shooting at him, just yet, so Stringer slowly headed back to the rail siding, as he considered his options. He didn't really care for any of them all that much.

That Jones had been sent after him was obvious. Jones had told him, not Pathe News, to get out of town. But before that it seemed just as obvious someone had gone out of the way to see the French film makers never got to this town in the first place. Had he not been with them, they might well be stuck out on the desert at this very moment. As he strode on, he reviewed everything that had happened since he'd joined the French outfit along the way. Leaving aside the fun he'd had, next to getting here by passenger coach, it seemed obvious that they'd have wound up in San Diego if he hadn't been along. That part could have been just a dumb mistake. But he couldn't see how leaving even a load of railroad ballast up a spur the railroad wasn't using could have been anything but deliberate. The Pathe crew would still be stuck there if, again, they hadn't had someone along who knew how to get 'em unstuck. So it was possible someone wanted him out of the way less for personal reasons than to have a better chance at . . . doing what, to those poor furriners?

LaRoche and his crew had made it to Columbus in time to film the big shoot-out. But if someone wanted the only one who could keep them out of trouble out of town, someone was still planning to *give* them some trouble. That had to be it. It made a heap more sense than chasing one reporter away from an event that was sure to be covered by all the other papers and wire services. Somebody was anxious to make sure, not that the battle was covered, but that it wouldn't be captured on *film*! No two eyewitnesses ever recorded events exactly the same way. The finer points could always be argued later. But a motion picture of an event could be run over and over, or even stopped in midmotion to study one important frame. Slickers relied on one split second to deal a card dirty or stuff a rabbit in a hat while everyone was looking the other way. He, she, or it would play hell doing that with one or more cameras cranking to record the whole show. But what in thunder could anyone be out to *hide*? The whole notion of a battle staged as public entertainment was just plain loco to begin with. Neither side could be out to hide the fact they were dumb as hell, could they?

But now that he suspected it was Pathe, not him, someone was really out to stop, Stringer started walking faster. For it was not only his duty to warn old La-Roche, he was also chilled to the bone. Besides, he'd told Claudette he might come back, and there was nothing like some sex to warm one's bones.

He approached the private car on the siding from its front end, simply because that was the end he spotted first in the darkness of the yards. He was mildly surprised to see a slit of light between the thick curtain and sill of Claudette's window. It was late and it was nice to see she'd left a light in her window for him after turning in. Then he froze in midstride with a puzzled frown and cocked his head to listen. He heard the same male voice repeat its requests and, again, the woman in there with him protested, "Oh, no, not in there! Your pee pee is just too big for my poor little poo poo, Mister Bennet!"

Stringer grimaced and started to turn away, muttering, "So much for leaving lights in windows. And to think I was too true-blue to take that tobacco shop gal up on her offer, faithful fool that I was."

Just then he heard her moan, "Oh! Yessss! That's just the way I like it!" and Stringer had to sneak closer, even though he knew he was playing the lovesick fool with a two-timing gal he'd never expected to marry up with, anyways.

But as he played Peeping Tom by standing on his toes with his eyes at the level of the narrow slit, Stringer found his teeth gritting harder than they had any right to, as he watched the fat ass of some fat dude he'd never seen before bouncing in the lamplight with Claudette's mesh-stockinged legs wrapped lovingly around his thick waist. Only, on second glance, it wasn't old Claudette or any other gal who'd ever betrayed him before. The strange fat boy was rutting ridiculously with a pneumatic dumb blonde who, despite her moans of passion, went right on chewing her gum with an expression of bored distaste.

So Stringer had to forgive Claudette, even as he tried to figure out why she'd lent her compartment to strangers with American accents.

Stringer moved along the side of the cars to the windows of the lit-up main salon. He peered in to see the same familiar interior, loaded buffet and all. Only the folk lounging about inside were unfamiliar to him. The gents came in all shapes and sizes. The three gals in there were all good lookers with mighty tempting figures. You could tell because none of 'em had all that much on, and one was seated in an old gray gent's lap, running her fingers through what was left of his hair as he slobbered at the straps of her thin chemise with his gums.

"Highjack?" pondered Stringer as he eased toward the rear platform with his gun out, peering around for some sign of the armed guards he expected to find. But there didn't seem to be any. What kind of orgiasts would commandeer a private car, do Lord only know what to its original passengers, and simply act as if they owned the whole shebang?

There was only one way to find out. Stringer mounted the platform, slid the rear door open, and stepped boldly in to fire a shot into the floor and yell, "Freeze, you bitches and sons thereof! Who the hell are you, and what have you done to the Pathe crew that's supposed to be here?"

The men, naturally, froze. One of the gals waved her glass at him and observed, "He's cute. Isn't that hat adorable?"

The old man with the young gal in his lap swallowed hard and then got brave enough to tell Stringer, "You're in the wrong pew if you work for Pathe, cowboy. This is the private car of the one and original Matt Bennet of Cosmopolitan Productions. You've seen our shorts, of course?"

A gal who wasn't wearing any shorts under her short shift modestly added, "I'm one of the Bennet Beauties."

Stringer tried to keep scowling. It wasn't easy. "I never accused anyone here of working for Pathe," he said. Then he stared about at the mahogany and brass fixtures less certainly as he insisted, less surely, "This sure looks like the same car."

The fat man who'd been trying to cornhole the gum-chewing blonde in Claudette's compartment came out wrapped in a big turkish towel, to demand, "What's going on out here, dammit?"

Then he noticed Stringer, or rather the smoking six-gun in his hand. So he added, "All right, we'll pass the hat for you. But I warn you, you'll never get away with this, Jesse James."

Stringer said, "I'm not out to rob anyone. I'm out to rescue some kidnapped French folk. I left them here, alive and well, just long enough to go into town for some tobacco and . . ."

"You got lost." Matt Bennet cut in with a laugh, adding, "That other motion picture crew is parked down the siding a few spaces, you idiot. We got here from Hollywoodland first, so the bunch from Pathe was lucky to find any siding left. Don't take my word for it. Go see for yourself, chump." Then he pointed at a spicy brunette with big tits and a bee-stung lower lip to say, "It's your turn, now, Flora. I just thought up a swell pose I'd like to see you in."

So she shrugged and followed him out of sight as Stringer sheepishly lowered his six-gun. The old cuss with the gal in his lap cackled and remarked, "Ain't he something? Takes at least five women a day to steady his nerves enough to direct a day's shooting. He's pretty good at that with his pants on, though."

Stringer nodded soberly and said, "I've seen his two reelers. They seem more innocent than his life off-camera. Are you folk here to film that comedy between Villa and Terrazas?"

The dirty old man cackled again and said, "Why, no, we just wanted some time on location with our prettier contract players. You're right about it being a comedy, if it ever comes off. First, they told us the battle was to be tomorrow. Now, they say they can't be sure. Pancho

Villa seems to be sulking in his dressing room about something. We're giving him just seventy-two hours to put up or shut up. You say you're here with Pathe?"

Stringer replied, "Not exactly. I take it you arrived so far ahead of us attached to the train from L.A. we somehow missed?"

The old coot shrugged and told him, "So far, you haven't missed much. Would you mind putting that dumb gun away?"

Stringer began to reload, instead, as he asked, "Who might this be who keeps changing the show bill on you? Have you made a deal with either Mex side?"

The old man shook his balding head to explain, "The army has the border closed until further notice. Things on this side are being managed by Pickins Enterprises. You don't know much if you haven't heard of Tex Pickins. He promotes bare knuckle boxing, bull fights, rodeos, all sorts of blood sports west of the Big Muddy. Used to work with Buffalo Bill 'til they had some sort of falling out over gate receipts."

"In other words he's a shady character." Stringer nodded. It was not a question. But the old cameraman or whatever nodded and replied, "He's been known to cut a few corners. But there's no way he can cheat us if this battle he's promoting is a fake. We made our own deal with the township of Columbus. If the battle comes off, we'll film it. If it don't, we won't. Pickins tried to shake down our young boss for rights to film the show. But you have to get up early to slicker Matt Bennet."

"I noticed he looks out for himself," Stringer observed dryly, adding, "So it's Pickins the promoter who keeps changing the time of the performance on you?"

"On us and everyone else." The old coot replied, "If those greasers don't get going, the crowd may start its own war with Mexico. Do you know they're asking a dollar a beer here in Columbus right now?"

Stringer said he was glad he didn't drink much and backed out to see if he could get some free wine while he found out who was trying to slicker whom around here. He quickly crunched down the siding feeling foolish, when he saw that he had, in fact, made a dumb mistake. The Pathe car was right where he'd left it. When he climbed aboard, he was just in time for a night cap with Claudette and a few other night owls. Old LaRoche had turned in already. He didn't ask with whom. When he brought them up to date on the Hollywoodland outfit up the siding, with Claudette translating, one of the French cameramen opined that the mystery of their earlier misadventures had been solved. Matt Bennet was known to be one ruthless operator, as it came out in French. But when Stringer asked if their rival had ever been accused of more serious sins than sodomizing would-be actresses, they had to allow, after some argument back and forth, that, so far, Bennet had never been accused of hiring assassins. "Bribing those railroad workers to how you say sidetrack us sounds just like one of his droll *practique* jokes," said Claudette, "He once paid a newspaper chain to rephrase show bills so that everyone came to see one of his comedies under the impression the drama of a rival would be playing on the same bill, rather than the theatres they had booked. Mais a species of thug hired to pick a serious fight with you, that could get someone sent to prison, non?"

Stringer shrugged and said, "Nobody who hires a gun expects to get caught, if his gun's any good. But before we accuse Bennet of even aiming custard pies this way, we'd best be certain he's the only gent with pies to throw. If *he* heard about the battle and *you* heard about the battle, who's to say how many *others* in the same business heard about it? We didn't know Matt Bennet was on the scene until just now. I'd best scout about some more before bedtime.''

"Mais, Stuart," Claudette protested, "I thought it *was* about that time."

"It's barely midnight," Stringer insisted, "and at the rate things are going, everyone may wind up sleeping late. Anyone serious about taking motion pictures ought to be parked somewhere in these same yards. It'll only take me a few minutes to find out who else is here."

Then he helped himself to some wine and ducked back outside. He didn't roll another smoke as he moved out to the service road to see if he could make out the layout of the yards better in the dim light. Dim light was no place to light a smoke when you had to study on who else might be poking about in the same. He felt halfway sure the one hired gun he'd taken out had been working alone. Nobody as easy to take out as Jones should have been working alone unless he had to. But it was better to be safe than sorry and so, until he had some notion as to what in thunder this was all about, he meant to act as if he was up against the whole Wild Bunch again.

From the service road, he just couldn't tell how many cars in all were parked along that double-siding, let alone how many might be just box cars or private cars with their lights out. He was fixing to move in for a car by car tally when the Mexicans in the noisy Maxwell putted across the tracks and swung his way. He knew he stood exposed to their headlamps as the beams swept over him. So he just stayed put and kept his gun hand polite as he waited for them to pass on by.

They didn't. The big Maxwell slammed on its brakes and slid to a dusty stop between Stringer and the yards,

which were the only cover. As Stringer braced himself
for a midnight game of "Tu Madre" with a bunch of
drunks, the side door flew open and one said, "Get in,
Stringer. We have been searching all over town for you.
Is it not fortunate we caught up with you at last?"

Having no other choice, Stringer got in, as he numbly wondered just how fortunate this was going to be for
him.

But they didn't even take his gun. So he figured his
boots were at least as safe for now, as they made room
for him in the rear seat, or tried to. It was hard for three
full-grown men to sit side by side when at least two of
them wore several cartridge belts, carried Winchesters,
and two or more six-guns, each. Stringer casually
hitched his own .38 to ride his right thigh and left his
hand on the grips just as casually, as he politely asked
where they might all be headed. The one who'd ordered
him to get in jovially replied, "We have to cross the
border well to the west. They got gringo soldados patrolling up and down the line, both ways, pero not too
far."

"We're on our way to Mexico?" Stringer asked in
English. While his Spanish was probably as good as
their own, there were times when it was smart to play
dumb.

The burly bandito in command replied in Spanish,
"Where else, and for why are you playing gringo games
with us? Have you forgotten me since last we met south
of the border, my rurale-shooting scribe?"

Stringer peered closer. Then he tried, "You were
serving as Villa's lieutenant that time?"

The burly Mex laughed boyishly and replied, "I am a
colonel, now. Pancho, he has promoted himself to the

rank of General. So I spit on lieutenants. You can call me Hernan, though. We fight for *democracia*, and I was never stuck up to begin with."

Stringer replied that he'd heard their cause was just and tried to keep track of where they were as the Maxwell bounded off across the rolling desert, not bothering to go around the clumps of prickly pear cactus it encountered in the darkness. He started to ask Hernan how they'd come by this modern means of transportation, and decided not to. It was tough to talk and bounce so high at the same time, and he really didn't want to know who they'd stolen the motor car from. He knew they frowned on being described as bandits and he owed it to his paper to report the truth, short of getting himself killed.

When they finally dipped down into a wash and the engine died trying to haul them up the far slope, Stringer suggested, "You might be using too much choke, muchachos."

Hernan growled, "Choke? Choke? Hey, Pablo, have you been choking somebody?"

To which the man at the wheel could only reply in a fatalistic tone, "Of course not. I have been having enough of a time just driving this estupido machine. How do you choke one? It sounds like a good way to make it behave, no?"

Stringer explained. He wasn't too surprised to learn they'd been driving in low gear with full choke all this time. Hernan told him to get behind the wheel if he knew so much, so Stringer did. Pablo got out to crank. That much he knew about lost, strayed, or stolen motor cars. All four of them seemed delighted and surprised that Stringer, once he had everyone aboard, was able to back up, rev the engine to full power, and take the far bank easily before he threw the transmission into second gear. When he asked which way to steer, Hernan chuckled, told him just to keep going, and added, "You must have done something to this thing. It's making a lot less noise, even though it's moving faster than before."

Stringer said it was just a knack. He was too polite to say it was a wonder they'd been moving at all, since they hadn't opened the choke or shifted gears since they'd found it parked that way. He knew they'd likely stolen it in New Mexico. The country to the south was even less civilized, and Maxwells were a rarity anywhere this far from any good-sized town.

When they came to another wash and Hernan said to just follow it south across the imaginary line that constituted the border, Stringer stopped, but left the engine running as he got out to trim the oil-fired head lamps.

When Hernan asked why, as he climbed back in, Stringer explained, "I just hate to get machinegunned. Some pretty good army units are watching for either side to invade Los Estados Unidos. I can see the white sand ahead without head lamps. So let's make them *guess* where we are. Twin headlamps can't be mistaken for anything else on or near the border. How did you muchachos drive this rig up here to begin with?"

Hernan shrugged and said, "Was daylight. You sure are smart for a gringo, Stringer. How many times have you jumped the border before this, eh?"

Stringer chuckled and replied, "As seldom as I can help it. That time we met over near the big bend was an accident. I was helping friends hunt stolen cows. We weren't paying all that much attention until those rurales jumped us to ask if we had entry visas, or pocket money."

Hernan sighed and said, "Si, was a grand running gunfight you were enjoying when you rode into us and *we* got all the pocket money in the end." He turned to his comrades to tell them, "This one knows how to deal with Los Rurales. He can nail them shooting backwards at full gallop, better than most pistoleros pick off bottles on a fence."

Thinking back to the last time they'd met inspired Stringer to ask, "Speaking of rurales, Hernan, how come there don't seem to be any around here right now? The U.S. Cav knows about your battle with Terrazas. They're even setting up moving picture cameras to film the fun and games. So doesn't Mexico have lawmen any more?"

"Private fight," Hernan said flatly, "Terrazas hates Pancho's guts. Pancho would piss on the grave of Terrazas' father, if anyone knew who that bastard's father was. Los Rurales know both sides would turn on them if they interfered in an affair of honor. Is all set up. Pancho will explain his battle plans to you. He said he wants you riding at his side because you write nice things about him. He gets very angry when gringo reporters call him a bandit. In that story you wrote about us, you said that we were only giving the government its just desserts. What are just desserts?"

"I wrote it only stood to reason that when a government abused its people beyond endurance they had the right and, indeed, the duty to fight back. My people tried to tell that to an English king one time. He didn't listen, either."

Hernan brightened and said, "I see. You say our Pancho is like your own George Washington, eh?"

"Well, within reason," Stringer muttered.

An hour later, they rolled into Pancho Villa's camp

set in the foothills of the dry Hatchet Range that brooded above the Chihuahua wastelands to the east.

The George Washington or Puma of Northern Mexico, depending on whom one asked, was making no great secret of his whereabouts, judging from all the night fires and guitar music. At Hernan's direction, Stringer stopped in front of a tent George Washington would have been proud of. As they all piled out, Pancho Villa nee Doroteo Arango, came out of his headquarters tent to greet them, wearing a broad smile and an adelita, or camp follower, on one arm. Villa was a husky gent in his late twenties or early thirties with pleasant peasant features and a trusting smile belied by Indian eyes that didn't seem to miss much. He told the girl clinging to him to go find a friend in case his Amigo from El Norte wanted to get married. Then, as she flounced off, Villa took Stringer by the hand to lead him inside, saying, "I am glad you will be riding with me, mañana. Some are sure to say I double-crossed a double-crosser. I want you there for to write everything down right."

Villa sat Stringer at a map table, and moved to the far side of the tent to pour two tumblers of tequila before sitting himself down. Stringer picked up his drink as he glanced down at the map. It was a U.S. Survey chart of the area around Columbus. He didn't ask how the guerrilla chief had gotten his own copy. Villa obviously knew how to read maps, judging from the lines he'd been penciling on it in red and blue. The blue positions were clearly his. Enemy positions were drawn in red by most military leaders. Terrazas would have his own maps colored the opposite way, if he was planning as hard as Villa.

The young Mex leader raised his own tumbler to

mutter, "Drink up. That bullshit with the lemon and salt is for tourists. We got lots to talk about and maybe you shouldn't get married tonight, with the day we face at dawn. That cabrone, Terrazas, has outdone himself this time as a shit-eating liar of lies. But I have my own spies out, and so mañana we shall see who is shitting whom, eh?"

Stringer took a sip of liquid fire. He couldn't have swallowed more than a sip at a time without letting his feeling show, and put the tumbler aside to get out his notebook as he said, "I think we'd better begin at the beginning, ah, General."

"To you I am always Pancho," Villa said, "I was born in the Year Of Our Lord, 1877, as private property. Don Arturo Lopez y Negrete owned the clothes on our backs as well as the land we had to work for him. Is not true that I was born in the Rio Grande as some have written. Don Arturo called his big hacienda Rios Grandes. I do not know why. Was all dry and my mother had to pay for our water. You know how the peonage system works, no?"

Stringer hadn't meant for him to start *that* far back, but he nodded and said, "Sure. We call it sharecropping in parts of my country. Landlord loans his tenants land and provisions to make a crop, only, from year to year, they never make enough to pay off what they owe him, so . . ."

"Was not working por nada, like my father and his fathers before him, that made me kill." Villa cut in, continuing, "Was the other bad things grandees think they can do to their peones as well. I had a sister. I do not wish to tell you her name, now that it has been dishonored. I was in prison when it happened. I had been flogged and locked up for trying to find work on another hacienda. While my sister was unprotected, she was raped by the son of Don Arturo. His name was Leonardo. I have to laugh at this when I think of how bravely he faced me when I demanded satisfaction. He refused to fight me mano a mano. He said hombres of his class did not stoop to dueling with peones. He was not too proud to stick his blue-blooded prick in a woman of the people, so I stuck my knife in him to spill his blue blood and, of course, they called that murder."

Villa swallowed a slug of tequila, then continued, "I ran off to the hills. A mounted rurale caught me. After that I had my own horse, guns, and a nice big rurale sombrero. I thought about seeking work as an honest charro. But every place I went, I saw posters screaming for my blood. My poor red Indio blood was now worth more to the grandees than before, eh? I thought, shit, if they get so excited over an hombre killing a rapist, I may as well give them something to be excited about, so I joined the band of Ignacio Parra. Was a good man, but you can put down that he was a bandit, like they say, if you like. Parra had even more Indio blood than me and was not as interested in justice. Back in the nineties, we just robbed everybody. About '95, we jumped a payroll coach. Was more heavily guarded than usual. Parra got shot. I got away. So now I was in command, and it was my idea for to give presents to the poor people as we rode. They had nothing to steal and once word got around that we were nicer than Los Rurales, it made it most difficult for Los Rurales to trail us. Since then, other muchachos mistreated by the grandees have rushed for to join us. I turn away more recruits than I have arms for. The army you see outside is good. Even our adelitas are more tough than the hired guns of Terrazas. He knows this. That is why he means for to double-cross us when we meet him for to put on the battle."

Stringer cocked a curious eyebrow and said, "Hold on, I got both ears open but I'm missing something, Pancho. You'd best tell me more about that battle you're fixing to have. No offense, but it sounds sort of dumb to me. I'm no military genius, but it seems suicidal on the part of both sides. All the battles I've ever read about involved such considerations as surprise, positions of advantage and such."

Villa snorted and said, "Carramba, I know that. So does that coward, Terrazas, even though he has not had half my experience as a hero. We *were*, how you say, fighting by the book until this Americano fight promoter, Pickins, approached us with his offer. Both sides could use the money and, in truth, the breathing spell. So we made a truce, just long enough for to stage the battle, only now..."

"I get it." Stringer cut in with an incredulous grin. "It's to be a *fixed fight*, just for tourist consumption, with a lot of noise and nobody really getting hurt amid the clouds of gunsmoke, right?"

Villa nodded morosely and replied, "We even got the blanks and smoke bombs from the promoters. Pickens said was all right for both sides to carry off their wounded as long as some of us fell down. The gringo showmen said to make it look good because some moving picture cameras would be there, and..."

"That's it!" Stringer cut in. Actually to himself. He saw Villa was confused and quickly explained, "Someone's been trying to prevent Pathe News from recording the event. They're good. The camera does not lie and some dead soldado breathing while he's supposed to be lying dead would be a matter of record, long after he died for real. Tex Pickins has been accused of staging less dramatic bouts. He can't afford to have his face exposed, so . . ."

"Is not a farce no more." Villa cut in, explaining, "I told you I got ears in Terrazas' camp. What good are adelitas if they do not really love you, eh? Nobody has to worry about soldados just playing dead, mañana. Terrazas plans to open up on us with live ammunition as we charge with blanks. Only guess what's really going to happen."

Stringer grimaced and said, "Ouch! But won't both sides take one hell of a heap of casualties, shooting it out face to face for real?"

"Sure," Villa replied.

Then he half rose to place a brown and surprisingly delicate finger on the map between them as he went on, "Here is that circus grandstand built for·to watch the amusing brown monkeys perform. A mile of concertina wire has been strung along the border to keep us in our place. East and west of the stands, Tio Sam will have posted plenty of his own troopers and a couple of batteries of machineguns. So neither side has to worry much about that flank."

Villa slashed a north-south line to the east of the scrawl he'd used to indicate the barbed wire along the border as he continued, "Terrazas' private army will no doubt line up about here. They are all vaqueros with a sense of adventure or a love of money. I mean to *show* them war for fun and profit. They will all be mounted, expecting us to be firing blanks and lobbing smoke grenades as they charge grandly past the viewing stands intending to slaughter us. Most of my pobrecitos still have to fight on foot. Is hard to keep horses in desert country, even when you can steal enough for everybody.

I'll position the riders I have to the south, on our right flank. Your gringo troops will have the kindness to guard my left flank as I advance my infantry in a skirmish line. As the enemy rides down on them, they will hit the dirt and take careful aim from prone positions. The vaqueros they will be spilling are not real soldados. They will break as they discover there is more to War than wine, women and parades. As they reel back, my own massed cavalry will take them on their south flank to drive them north against the tangled barbed wire Tio Sam was good enough to provide me. Your people seated in the stands should see all the blood and slaughter they paid to see, up close, eh?"

Stringer whistled and replied, "More than they bargained for if they don't duck! Those U.S. Army troops are certain to open up on all concerned when they see two Mexican armies headed right at 'em. We're talking about Krag rifles along with machinegun fire, Pancho!"

Villa nodded and said, "I'm counting on that. A lot of my foot soldier are still carrying old single-shot Springfields, or even muzzle loaders."

Stringer shook his head and insisted, "Never mind your ordnance. What kind of a medical corps do you have? A Mex is a Mex to a rattled army machinegunner going rat-tat-tat, so you're bound to get a heap of your own men mowed down in the process."

Villa nodded soberly. "I know. I got no medical corps. We shoot the wounded of both sides, unless they can still march. You would be surprised how far a man with a bullet in him can march, when he knows he *has* to."

Stringer swallowed another slug of tequila. The comic opera aspects of Latin American warfare seemed to be losing a heap of humor in the translation. *This* clown sounded *serious* about the subject.

The adelita Villa had sent to find a friend came back in with another girl. The one Stringer was supposed to "marry" was younger, a lot prettier, and had her hands tied behind her. Lest that not be enough, a couple of grinning soldados had her covered with their drawn six-guns. Before Stringer could say he preferred his women willing, Villa shot a sharp glance at the plain homespun cotton smock and bright red sash the sullen beauty had on. Then he told the other adelita, "I sent you to fetch us a *woman*. This is no woman. Can't you see she's *Yaqui*?"

One of the guards chimed in with, "She must have wanted to join your army, General. We caught her skulking in the cactus just outside of camp."

Villa muttered something dreadful about his follower's family tree, suggesting they never should have come down from it, before he addressed the Indian captive in a tongue that reminded Stringer of Paiute, even though he couldn't follow it. The Yaqui girl shot daggers back at Villa with her smouldering sloe eyes as she spat back at him in the same dialect. But whatever he was saying seemed to calm her down somewhat, though she never stopped glaring at him as he nodded, switched back to Spanish, and said, "Her pony gave out on her in the desert. She was trying to steal one of ours when you caught her. Take her out to the remuda and let her pick out a good mount. We'd better give her a couple of canteens of water as well. Then let her go with God. I just told her what will happen to her if she does not go straight home to her own people."

One of the guards frowned uncertainly and asked,

"You wish for us to reward this ladrona with one of our own mounts, General?"

Villa growled, "Do you question your general's orders? Do as I say, muy pronto. Can't you see I'm busy here?"

The adelita and two soldiers exchanged confused stares, then started to lead the Indian girl out. She moved with them as far as the exit slit. The she turned to stare back at Villa as if she was examining a bug on a pin. She took a deep breath then, with an obvious effort, she snarled, "Como se llama, Mejicano?"

To which Villa replied with a shrug, "Villa, Pancho Villa. Adios y mucho gusto, Señorita."

She looked more insulted than pleased as she grudgingly muttered, "Gracias, Pancho Villa." Then she was gone.

Villa smiled wearily at Stringer and said, "I've told them not to be rude to the Yaqui. God knows, I have enough on my hands as it is. She says my men didn't dishonor her, thank God. Let's hope that's the end of it."

Stringer said, "I wouldn't want the Yaqui mad at me if I could avoid it. I understand that can be tough, even when you speak their tongue."

Villa smiled modestly and explained, "I spoke to her in my own Chihuahua dialect. Is close enough. As you just heard, they can speak Spanish when they want to. They just don't want to. The Yaqui claim to be leftover Aztecs who never gave in to Cortez. I think they are full of shit, but who wants to argue with such a ferocious tribe of lunatics and what are you grinning about?"

Stringer went on smiling thinly, as he replied, "I'm just trying to understand you. One minute you're talking about killing your own wounded and the next you're going out of your way to be gallant to a female captive. She was in your power, and was mighty pretty."

Villa looked disgusted and said, "Carramba, what use is a woman who is sure to bite it off for you the first chance she gets? Most of the women in Mexico *want* to go to bed with me. For I, Pancho Villa, shall march into Mexico City as the savior of my country by the end of this decade, or, maybe two decades. I got some fighting to do, first."

Stringer nodded soberly and said, "That's for damned sure at the rate you're going. We were talking about you getting half of your boys killed off in that battle with another gang, as I recall."

Villa sat back down and helped himself to more tequila as he insisted, "A general who thinks he can win battles without losing any men has no business sending men into battle. Is no way to fight a war without both sides losing men. The only way you win is by making the other side lose *more*. Have you forgotten your own General Grant at Shiloh?"

Stringer stared incredulously at the chunky mestizo in the bandit outfit before replying, "That was a mite before my time, and yours as well, unless you're fibbing about your age."

Villa shook his head and said, "A good soldado studies well-fought battles, no matter when they happened. I have had some history books read to me. Your Grant was my kind of soldado. The war you gringos had among yourselves would have been over sooner if they'd put him in command earlier. Your McClellan was a sissy. He could not bear to see his tin soldados damaged. At Shiloh, the other side lay in ambush for Grant. Was a good ambush. Everyone but Grant knew he was getting the shit kicked out of him. But when they begged him to retreat, he told them not to be so stupid. He said to add up the figures. The north had more than twice as many troops as the south at Shiloh. Now that the surprise was over, the bigger army had to win, if only they would stop talking about what was to be done and just *do* it. You know what happened then, of course."

Stringer nodded soberly to reply, "Sure. It was one of the bloodier victories in a bloody war. Even his own troops called him Butcher Grant before it was all over."

Villa chuckled fondly and insisted, "But he *won*. He won for the simple reason that he kept killing Lee's men faster than Lee could replace them. War is not so complicated, once you make up your mind to cut out the shit and get down to *business*."

He waved a hand expansively at the interior of his tent but must have meant the camp outside as he continued, "My people have been trying to overthrow Diaz since before either of us could say Da Da. Every time a man of the people has risen, Diaz has crushed him like a cockroach. He even *calls* us cockroaches. Little brown, unimportant creatures. He is so proud of being half Spanish. But I, Pancho Villa, know how to fight him. He is not a military genius. He just has a big army and a ferocious police force. He has to recruit replacements, the same as me. I told you I got more muchachos anxious to join my army than I have arms and equipment for. Each time I win a battle I get more arms and my losses matter less. *Padre Tiempo* rides on my side, as well. I am still young and brave. Each day El Presidente grows older and less sure of himself. Give me just ten years. Maybe a little more. You will see."

Stringer sighed and said, "You must be part Chihuahua. Nobody but an Indian would have that much patience, and what if they kill you first, Pancho?"

Villa shrugged and said, "Is not important. I have taught a lot of cockroaches how to fight my way. Someone will just take my place. Mexico will be free because she wishes to be free. Is as simple as that."

CHAPTER
EIGHT

Considering how little sleep he'd gotten, Stringer was wide awake in the cold gray light of dawn as he rode at Pancho Villa's side into the sunrise. He was also as hungry as a bitch wolf. So was everyone else in the ragtag rebel army he was marching with. For Villa was against having breakfast on the day of any battle. He thought the gringo notion of feeding the troops a swell meal just before they went into action estupido. He'd asked Stringer what Americano medics did about a trooper gut-shot on a full stomach and Stringer had had to confess he didn't even want to think about it.

It was obviously all right to smoke, though. Every third or fourth man moving in line with them seemed to be puffing a big cigar. Stringer had already made notes on the cigar smoking grenadiers and what they were packing in those cotton rucksacks. The promoters of the show had issued them smoke cannisters. Villa had made them tamp in more powder and lots of horseshoe nails.

Stringer was riding on Villa's left, near the south end of the mile-long skirmish line, so there was nothing between Stringer and the border but a thousand-odd wild-eyed Mexicans on foot and loaded for bear. It was tempting. But what the hell, Sam had sent him to cover the battle and this had to be about the best seat in the house. He was mounted on a frisky bay charger that also carried the brand of Los Federales, or the Mexican regular army. Villa's pony was white, of course. On the far side of the somewhat bloody-minded liberator rode a skinny twelve year old bugler and a teenaged guidon carrying a big red flag, just in case anyone mistook this outfit for anything but rebels. To the further south rode Villa's cavalry, if that was what one wanted to call about five hundred gents with ammo belts mummy-wrapped about their charro costumes. Stringer noticed that, like Villa himself, troop leaders seemed to favor American cowboy hats instead of the big floppy sombreros everyone else had on. When he asked his mentor if this was a badge of rank, Villa said, "Si. Is good for doing business in your country as well. When I am not doing battle with Terrazas' riders, as I mean to this morning, I sell a lot of his cows in Texas, sometimes Arizona, too. Your rangers do not seem to get as excited when they see their own kind of hats herding cows, eh?"

Stringer smiled thinly and observed, "Helps when you want to throw a community loop at a Texas cow as well, right?" To which Villa replied in an injured tone, "Is not true! I am not a *ladrone*, as my enemies say. I have never stolen anything on your side of the border. I have been tempted. Gringo banks are not nearly as well fortified as they have to be in this country. But how would it look for El Presidente to have a criminal record after I get to be El Presidente, eh?"

Stringer lit a fresh smoke as he digested that. Then he asked, "Do you really expect to get that far, Pancho?" To which Villa replied with simple dignity, "Why not? God knows, my poor country has only had one honest government since we got rid of the damned

Spanish years and years ago, and Juarez was of Indian blood, no?"

"They say he was an educated lawyer as well." Stringer pointed out, in a cautious tone.

But Villa just said, "I can hire men of education to help me run the country, once I am in charge of it. Has any pencil pushing maricón ever come forward to fight Diaz for control? Carramba, they are content to kiss his ass. He treats well those he finds useful to him. It is us, the cockroaches, who have no other choice but to fight him."

Then he raised his free hand and reined in to peer ahead into the sunrise as he added, "Speaking of bugs . . ."

Stringer raised his own right palm to shade his eyes, or try to, as he did his best to read the dusty glare to the east. He made out the grandstands off to their left. The stands looked full, and some of the crowd seemed to be waving at them. A kid's balloon escaped to soar upwards as a black dot against the sunrise. Further out, lined up atop a gentle rise, he could just make out the other side. Villa had been right about them all showing up on horseback. They added up to a heap of horses, many more than Villa had mounted or afoot. The open ground between the two armies was gently rolling and harshly studded with clumps of prickly pear. Cactus only made good cover when there was more of it. It didn't stop bullets worth a damn.

Villa muttered something to his young bugler. The kid blew a call Stringer was unfamiliar with. But while he'd never been at the Alamo that time, he made an educated guess at "No Quarter" and, sure enough, a distant tinny bugle blew it right back at them. Then both buglers sounded the more familiar "charge," which was more like a brisk walk when one was riding with Villa. But as the ragtag infantry to his left advanced in a fairly well-dressed skirmish line, some of them already reaching for their nail bombs, Stringer couldn't help muttering, to nobody in particular, "Could I just sit this dance out?"

He glanced back over his shoulder. A quarter mile back, an even longer skirmish line of adelitas was following the advance on foot. Not even a rider's adelita rated her own pony. But some of the gals were packing rifles as well as their soldier's packs. At the rate the two front lines were moving at one another, they seemed fated to meet just about in front of the grandstand. Stringer knew that up in their safe seats, his own kind of folk would be cracking jokes about the comical greasers putting on a show for them. From the seat *he* had, it didn't look half as funny.

Villa reined in on a small rise, signalling his riders to halt as the foot soldiers kept going. Stringer needed no invitation to rein in with them at a safer range. Then he had to reconsider how safe that might be when the kid holding the big red banner emitted a harsh coughing sound and fell off his pony, flag and all.

The young bugler dropped lightly to the ground to pick up the red banner as Villa muttered, "What did I tell you? Live ammunition, the sons of unwashed nuns and defrocked priests!"

Something whizzed past Stringer's hat, humming like a metal hornet. He winced and shouted, "They have us ranged, and they know who you are, Pancho! Do we really have to wave that flag at them? Can't we let 'em guess?"

Villa shook his head sternly and said, "Is the banner of our *libertad*. Long may it wave!" Then the small boy waving it took a round in the head and did a back flip off his pony, carrying the flag to the dust with him.

Villa shouted, "Enough of this military courtesy. They are charging at full gallop, so let's take them on the flank as they reach our infantry!"

Nobody argued, but it was easier said than done. For even as Stringer tried to ride along with Villa, the whole world filled with sun-hazed gunsmoke. Villa's foot soldiers used black powder in both their rifles and nail bombs, and the riders charging down on them blazed away with black powder, too. From time to time, Stringer's pony ran over somebody or he'd spot somebody rising above the smoke like a rag doll tossed skyward by a wayward child. But other than that, he was just riding blind through one hell of a lot of noise. And even as one part of him tried not to shit his pants, another part of him kept wondering, with amazing calm, whether battles were always this confusing. When you read about battles in books, they made a hell of a lot more sense. When you were *in* one, they scared the shit out of you. He'd thought those times in Cuba during the war with Spain had just confused him because he wasn't one of the officers who knew what was going on. But as he rode right next to one side's commander, it seemed obvious that Villa was just as confused as the rest of them. Yet the chunky Mex seemed to be having a swell time, from the way he was shouting orders. Villa was likely more used to this bullshit, Stringer decided, just as a uniformed rider emerged from the dazzling mist with a cavalry saber raised to clobber both of them.

Stringer didn't like that at all. So he drew his .38 and blew the cavalryman over the rump of his horse, sword and all, to hear Villa shouting, "Gracias. Hey! Was that a federale?"

Stringer didn't get the chance to offer a comment on the snappy olive tunic the jasper had been wearing at the time of his demise. Villa screamed, "A double cross on a double cross! Terrazas changed places with the fucking *army*! Vamanos, muchachos! Is time to live to fight another day!"

That was easier said than done, too. As Villa led the retreat at full gallop, or *thought* that was what he was doing, Stringer closed in to shout, "Wrong way!" as somewhere in the haze to the north a U.S. Army machinegun cleared its throat. "See what I mean?" Stringer added.

To which Villa could only answer, "I'll get them for this! Take the lead!"

Stringer did, even though it wasn't too clear where they ought to go, save for the fact that any direction but southwest seemed worse. Then things got worse. The federales opened up with the field artillery they'd brought along. One didn't have to be a military genius to see that Villa's side could only run for their lives. It was hard to tell, amid all that dust and gunsmoke, how many of his troops were escaping. Stringer's mount shied as it saw or smelled a pile of mangled remains on the lip of a shell crater ahead. Then they'd loped past and Stringer hadn't even tried to guess whether that had been two or four mangled bodies back there. A riderless pony passed on their left, inspired to outrun them by its empty saddle and trailing guts. A shell came down close, on the far side of Villa, who laughed bitterly and shouted, "They're just guessing. Keep going!" So Stringer did.

As the haze ahead cleared slightly, he spied an adelita in a dusty black dress running barefoot over torn earth and pulverized cactus. Without slowing, Stringer reached down to scoop her up with his free arm and deposit her behind him to ride pillion, clinging to him for dear life with her head pressed to the back of his jacket while she moaned, "Gracias, gracias, gracias!" like a busted gramophone.

A shell landed ahead to shower them all with dirt clods as they tore on through the mustard colored, cordite scented confusion. The next time Stringer could see his hand before his face he saw Villa had scooped up another frightened girl. The burly young Mex shouted, "Veer to the south. They know where our camp is, the triple-crossing, two-faced offspring of three-thumbed toads!"

"What about your followers?" asked Stringer, even as he reined south-southwest, according to the sky above.

"What followers?" Villa called back. "Can't you see they kicked the shit out of us? I get licked every time I fight the regular army, so far. Now is every cockroach for itself, no?"

That was the way it looked to Stringer. It hadn't been his army to begin with. Yet even as they rode like the wind in all directions, he seemed to be more worried about Villa's shattered and scattered followers than Villa himself was.

Horses had to be rested after they'd run a few miles. Horses had no sense about a lot of things. So even though the artillery barrage seemed too close for comfort to their northeast, they reined in for a breather when they found themselves in a prickly pear flat instead of out on open ground.

Nobody had ever explained pear flats to Stringer's satisfaction. Prickly pear just seemed to grow close together in little dry jungles or not at all. The ten or twelve foot walls of mushy cactus pads all around them afforded more cover from the human eye than bullets or even arrows. But as Villa cheerfully pointed out, you had to see a cabron to shoot at him, and both the army bay and his own white charger were badly winded after running so far under double loads. So they all got off and the two girls, without being told, commenced to feed and water the stock at the same time by peeling and feeding them pear pads. The cactus was not in fruit, so the four human fugitives were out of luck unless they were thirsty enough to chew what tasted like soapy sponges. Both saddles had canteens lashed to their swells. So Stringer asked the adelitas if they were thirsty.

They just looked at him. He could see they were both more Indian than Spanish. So it had likely been a dumb question. He'd been told by Miwok, back on the Mother Lode range where it rained more often, that white folk sure drank a lot of liquids.

The one Villa had rescued wasn't bad, if one liked one's women plump and moon-faced. The raggedy waif Stringer had saved was closer to what a white man considered pretty. When he handed her his pocket knife so she could peel cactus pads with less damage to her small, strong fingers, she demurely informed him she was called Felicidad and that she'd love him forever, even if he married some other adelita. He said he loved her, too, but to hold the thought for now. He turned back to Villa and said, "I think we made it, for the moment. Now what? Over the Hatchet Range into Hidalgo County, New Mexico? The border cuts south about thirty miles on the far side of the divide, you know."

Villa grimaced and said, "Of course I know. I got to

keep an eye on where I am, even when I don't want the other side to know. The last time I got licked I hid out in Texas for a while. But I don't wish to hide out in New Mexico. Would make me feel bad if Los Gringos there were nice to me. I don't like to kill anyone who has been nice to me, and New Mexico *owes* me, no?"

Stringer frowned dubiously to ask, "Owes you what, Pancho? I thought we just tangled with your own federales."

Villa swore and then growled, deep in his throat, "You must not call them *my* federales. Diaz owns them, along with the honor of their mothers. That town back there, Columbus, was in on it with Diaz, no?"

Stringer shook his head and said, "No. I was in Columbus when your segundo picked me up. They were selling tickets to watch you slug it out with Terrazas. They'd have been asking for more per seat had they expected the whole Mex Army to show up. You can't blame the town of Columbus for what happened just now."

But Villa insisted, "Sure I can. Someday I go there back to get me some lying gringos. But not yet. First I got to put my army back together."

Stringer smiled incredulously and said, "I hate to be a wet blanket, *General*. But don't you think we'd better worry about the army on our heels before we worry about anything else?"

Villa said, "You could be right. I don't hear them shelling, now. They'll be mopping up the battlefield right now. Then, as always, they'll spread out for to track down the survivors."

They all heard a distant pistol shot. Stringer said, "I follow your drift. Where do we go from here if you don't like mountain scenery?"

Villa said, "The scenery up there is nice. The Yaqui are not. I think we better head due south, sticking to the flats for a hundred miles or so."

Stringer whistled softly and observed, "It's your country. But I hope you know what you're doing, Pancho. We're talking mighty dry country at the best of times, and this year you seem to be having a drought even *you* guys call dry!"

Villa shrugged and said, "We can't stay here. They know about pear flats, too. You are right about the drought. Won't be no water in the Rio Casas Grandes a few hour's ride to the south. But maybe Los Federales will expect us to make for there. Better we follow the aprons of the foothills south. Lousy country for man or beast and, once we get a few days upstream, might be a little water in the river bed."

But the plump adelita Villa had saved, whose name was Ynez, took a deep breath, then dared to say, "Not for nearly a week in the saddle, my Hero. You speak of country I know well. I ran away from a hacienda near the headwaters of the Casas Grandes because my mistress beat me and my master was almost as bad in bed. The river comes down from the Sierra Madre, even in summer, only to sink into the sand as it runs north almost to the border and, in a very wet year, hairpins around to water a desert playa to the south. In dry weather like this, the river bed is dry as a bone north of Los Gringos who have a dam across the river, see?"

Villa said, "Let's mount up. If the journey is dry and difficult, Los Federales may not follow us too far."

So a few minutes later they'd broken through the far side of the pear flat to drift slow and steady through the cholla and greasewood, trying not to raise any dust, and looking back a lot.

To the north, the horizon was obscured by the slowly settling haze of battle. From time to time they still heard distant shots as yet another wounded survivor met a lonely end. Stringer knew he was just about as far south as he really wanted to be. It wasn't his fight, and he could no doubt make the border if he simply holed up somewhere until dark and took his chances alone. Then the girl clinging to him from behind murmured, softly, "Do you think we are going to be caught by Los Federales, mi soldado?"

To which he could only reply, "Not if I can help it. I'm not as casual about deserting my friends as some gents I could mention."

Sunset found them camped in a dry arroyo with not enough water in their canteens to mention. A fire was out of the question with federales scouting the desert for them and Yaqui haunting the purple crest to their west. Stringer knew their mounts needed the rest. But suggested, as they all sat around a sort of picnic blanket with no picnic on it, "If I was in charge, Pancho, I'd move out again around midnight. I've interviewed many an old Apache fighter and they all agreed it's best to ride by night and hole up by day in Apache country."

Villa snorted in disgust and said, "Apaches squat to piss. This is *Yaqui* country. They got eyes like cats. They fight better in the dark than any other time. If we've been spotted from the ridges to our west they are laying for us, right row, on the trail ahead. You let me worry about our pagan playmates, my gringo Apache fighter. Yaquis don't like to fight in the open with the sun revealing all their sins. They are formidable close range fighters, but lousy shots. Some of them still got bows and arrows. Is safer we ride by daylight, steering wide of any ambush sites, eh?"

"Won't that leave us exposed to any army patrols on the flats?" Stringer asked.

Villa replied with a yawn, "I spit in their mother's milk. Better to fight a hundred federales than one Yaqui woman. Yaqui women are really wicked."

The young mestiza woman snuggled against Stringer's left side gulped and softly asked, "What if they move in on us in the dark? "Madre de Dios," Villa muttered, "does everybody in this army want to be the general? I just told you Yaqui like to spring surprises. They do not like to *be* surprised. If they even know we are here, they know we got guns. Three pistols and my saddle carbine, anyway. They expect us to be on the alert, with at least one of us on guard, see?"

"Don't you think we ought to think about posting a night watch up on the rim, then?" Stringer asked.

To which Villa replied with another yawn, "For why? I just told you they expect us to. So why bother? You got to learn to relax between fights, muchacho. The secret of living as we must is to take it easy and enjoy life as much as you can, while you still got it. We have had a rough day. I could use a warm meal right now, too. But I got some tequila in my saddle bag and if we marry these two women we might not notice how hungry we are, eh?"

The two adelitas laughed expectantly. Stringer had to grin, but asked, "I've been meaning to ask you about that, Pancho. The last time we met you'd just married the alcalde's daughter, or said you had. Am I missing something in the translation? Where I come from the term means something more, ah, formal."

"Hey, I'm as formal as any damned gringo. You take

me for a caballero with no respect for women? I always marry women before I make love to them. Would not be decent to treat them like putas, see?"

"I'm trying to. I'm sure my readers will be interested in just how you go about it."

"Is simple. If a captain of a ship can marry men and women it stands to reason a *general* can. You two, hold hands. Ynez, give me your pretty little paw."

Stringer suddenly found his left hand gripped in both of Felicidad's brown hands as Villa said, "Bueno. I now pronounce us man and wife. You two, as well, Stringer."

Felicidad said she was so happy and kissed him. She kissed pretty good for such a simple country girl. When they came up for air Stringer laughed weakly, and asked Villa, "How many women does one man get to marry, according to your version of a religion I always assumed was more serious about such matters, Pancho?"

Villa said, "Was not a Catholic ceremony. Do I look like a priest? I got the idea from some Mormon settlers near Durango. They came down here to practice their most sensible marriage customs when your Utah became a state and started acting picky. I don't know much about Mormons. Some day I gotta take back all that land Diaz sold them. But I like the way they get married. It makes the women just as happy and is not so hard on the men, eh?"

Stringer laughed again and would have asked more questions about Villa's religious views, but the lusty Mex cut him off with "Let's go to bed, damn it. Can't you see I'm on my honeymoon?"

Felicidad nudged Stringer to murmur, "We had better move up a ways. I do not think they wish for us to watch." Villa rolled Ynez atop the blanket and proceeded to undress her, so Stringer got up, helped Felicidad to her feet, and led her and their pony around a bend in the sandy arroyo.

They didn't even have the tequila. But there was a bedroll strapped to the bay's saddle. Felicidad had been bouncing on it all day. He started to unlash it, feeling awkward. But she told him that was an adelita's job and shoved him aside to get right to work. She worked with practiced skill and had the bedding spread out before Stringer finished tethering the pony to a mesquite limb. As he turned, he saw her spread out on the blankets in the starlight, naked as a jay. He was beginning to see what Villa meant about taking life as it came on the owlhoot trail. He didn't want her to think him a sissy. He knew she couldn't really see his red face or dawning erection in this dim light, so he sat down beside her to shuck off his duds. It took him a lot longer, since he started out wearing more clothing than Felicidad. He rolled his gun rig up in his hat and placed it handy in the nearby sand with its grips pointing up for a sudden grab. By this time, she'd grabbed him, and it was pretty hard to begin with. So he grabbed her back and they were too busy to talk for a delirious spell. He hadn't known how much he needed the release until he came in her, hard. From the way she responded he knew she, too, was acting as much by instinct as amour. Poleaxed steers and men getting hung shot their wads with their last dying twitches, too. It was probably a reflex left over from before mammals had crawled out on dry land. it made sense for a fish to try for one last chance at breeding when it was dying or scared. But, since they were both human beings and weren't really dying, it felt a heap better to come together over and over until they just had to stop for breath.

Felicidad hugged him tight with her strong tawny limbs as she cooed, "Maria, Jose y Jesus, that was oh, so lovely, my husband!" And while he had to agree it sure beat dying, her words left him feeling somewhat low.

"I hope you understand it was Pancho's idea to say that about us, querida. I like you a lot. I even meant most of what I was saying, just now, but . . ."

"Do not burst my bubble." She cut in, adding with a sad little sigh, "I know what I really am to you. But even an adelita likes to dream, and we do have this one small slice of forever all to ourselves, no?"

He kissed her gently and replied, "It's about as nice a slice of eternity as I've had so far. I wasn't trying to hurt you. I was trying not to, when this forever sort of slips away on us."

She hugged him tighter and said, "I know. Make it last as long as such forevers ever can. I shall not shame you before your real woman, if she ever knows of this moment with an adelita."

He started to say he was single. But that could have been even tougher on her. So he asked, "Just what do you folk mean by an adelita? I know that's what they call you girls. But I don't see why. It sounds like a girl's name, not a military title."

She replied, "It *is* a girl's name, from a most sad corrida about the first Adelita and her soldado."

Then she rolled him on his back and got on top to slowly move her muscular young body up and down his shaft as she began to croon the folk song. She was right about it being sad. But he had no complaints about the way she was strumming, as the song went on and on about poor Adelita tending her soldado's wounds when he wasn't beating her or messing with other gals. The moral of the corrida, if there was one, seemed to be that Adelita and her namesakes were just what the doctor ordered as hardworking and hot-natured camp followers. This one started moving faster before she could get to the end of her song. So he rolled her over to finish right and never heard the end of "Adelita" if it had an end. He wasn't sure he cared to know. And later, as they shared a smoke, he asked her just what in thunder gals like her got out of trudging along behind their ragtag troops, unwed, unpaid, and sure to wind up dead, sooner or later.

Felicidad took a luxurious drag of Bull Durham, let it out with a sigh of animal pleasure, and asked, "What better life is there for a woman of peon birth in a country such as mine? Would you have me draw water and hew firewood for a lazy grandee woman who calls me her chica when she is not cursing me? I am still young and not bad-looking. I know men want me. Why should I be passed around as a toy by land owners, who do not respect me, when I can just as well give pleasure to men I admire? Is a hard life, sure, but is a free life and, someday, whether I live to see it or not, my people will own this country. Then won't the grandees be sorry they treated us like cockroaches instead of human beings!"

He took the smoke back, inhaled, and let it out as he thought about that. She'd told him not to burst her bubble, so he kept his thoughts to himself. Old Diaz couldn't last much longer, he knew. But then what? Would guys like Villa be any improvement? Diaz, himself, had started as a guerrilla leader under Juarez. He'd said he was a man of the people and he'd probably thought he was, until he'd been in power long enough to learn how power corrupts, and how nice it feels to be corrupted. It was going to take more than a man on a white horse to change things south of the border. The political hacks *north* of the border shit on the little guys whenever the little guys let 'em. The problem with folk down here was that they trusted any bozo willing to promise them a fair shake or, hell, just to get off their backs. He stared up at the uncaring stars and held Felicidad closer as he murmured, "I wish there was something I could do. I *like* your people, Felicidad. They ask so little. They get so little. I swear I can't see why they're so cheerful and friendly to anyone who isn't biting them on the leg."

She murmured, "You are not like other gringos. Some of them abuse us, too. Why do your people come down here to buy land and evict all the pobrecitos? Why do they call our brothers lazy greasers even though they seem most anxious to sleep with us? Why do they call us greasers? Do I feel greasy to you?"

He held her cool naked flesh closer to his own, aware he hadn't had a bath all that recently, as he assured her she felt just swell. "I don't think all of my people investing down here worry all that much about your feelings. Diaz advertises in the *Wall Street Journal*, offering cheap land, cheap labor, and no labor unions to worry about. Our own Teddy Roosevelt's started to fuss about our robber barons up north. I imagine they're just trying to do business as usual in a land where nobody gives a damn."

She said, "I give a damn. Someday I'm going to catch a stuck-up gringa and snatch her baldheaded. But you I like, tonight."

The next day they came upon the sometimes river. Ynez had been right about it running dry, this far north. The broad bed of the Casas Grandes formed a highway of sun baked adobe, with scrubby mesquite along either bank. Villa led them down into the bed, saying it was about time they did some serious riding. Stringer told him to speak for himself. Horses could get by on cactus pads, and chewing mesquite pods beat starving, but as they rode upstream toward the everdryer south, nobody but Stringer seemed to care where they were going, or if they'd ever get to eat again. The two adelitas seemed delighted to be riding pillion instead of trudging along behind them barefoot, carrying heavy packs. Stringer had to admire Villa and his breed. No matter what the fancier folk said about them, they were tough as hell. He was beginning to see why the government couldn't do much about their so-called bandit problem in northern Mexico.

It was Villa who spotted something on the far bank of the dry river bed and veered closer. Stringer saw the tracks before Villa pointed at them with a merry laugh and said, "Old Hernan must have got away in that fancy horseless carriage he stole. I wonder how he made it out of camp with all those shells coming down, eh?"

As they walked their mounts further upstream in line with the mysterious rubber tire tracks, Stringer said, "I'm not so sure. Those look more like motor truck tracks to me, Pancho. Have your federales started patrolling the desert in trucks, yet?"

Villa shrugged and said, "I wish you'd stop calling them *my* federales. I got my own army, see?"

Stringer blinked, stared ahead at the shimmering horizon to the south, and asked, "Where? No offense, but we seem to be all that's left, ah, General."

Villa shrugged and said, "Is not important. As long as I am still alive, my army still exists. I told you I got licked before. Last time, they killed everybody but me and Hernan. We had to work in Texas as vaqueros for a few months. Then we came back to regroup, see?"

Stringer replied, "Not hardly. Regroup what, if they'd just wiped you out?"

Villa's tone was that of an indulgent adult explaining the facts of life to a child as he said, "My army, of course. Look, in Chihuahua alone we got all the land owned by less than three thousand big shots. Terrazas alone owns half of it. That leaves two million, two whole million landless peon families, and my people raise big families. You think I got to work hard to re-cruit an army with Diaz working as my recruiting of-ficer?"

Stringer whistled. It was getting harder to do that as his lips kept getting drier. He didn't see anyone lining up around here, but he was beginning to get the picture. Felicidad had told him her kind felt they had nothing to lose, and she was one tough little gal. Villa's army was in his heart, or the hearts of his people. All they asked for was a rallying point and he still had that white horse, after all.

They rode in line with the truck tracks for a spell, then one of the adelitas commented on the buzzards cir-cling up ahead. Villa said, "I see them. They would not be up there if the thing they are watching was dead. You girls better stay here and hold the horses. Stringer and me will move in on foot to see what those birds are so interested in."

They all dismounted. The two men left the girls with the ponies in the sparse shade of the mesquites and fol-lowed the same shade up the dry river, guns ready. Stringer had his .38 out. Villa carried his cocked Win-chester at port arms while his two six-guns rode his broad hips. For close to a mile, the only sound was the crunch of their boot heels in the crusted adobe. Then they both froze as they heard a low agonised moan.

Finding where it was coming from took some doing. The dying man, or what was left of him, had crawled into the streamside brush to get out of the cruel sun. It hadn't really done him much good. Someone had stripped him to the buff. Then they'd cut off his nose and eyelids. Then they'd peeled the soles of his feet to turn him loose on the hot desert grit to see how far he could make barefoot. As the mutilated wretch heard them coming he screamed in terror and raised his blood and sand-caked face to stare their way, blindly, with his widely staring but sunblinded eyes. Villa said, in a conversational tone, "Yaqui. Not him, the ones who *caught* him."

Stringer raised his gun muzzle. Villa said, "No! Do you want them mad at us, too? This one's a federale. See how white his ankles are from cavalry boots? The Yaqui don't like federales, either. Let us hope I knew what I was doing when I turned that Yaqui girl loose the other night. Meanwhile, we'd better get back to our own girls, and those ponies."

Stringer protested, "We can't just leave him here like this!" To which Villa replied, coldly, "Why not? We didn't do it to him, and is not as if we owe his kind any favors. Los Federales have less imagination than the Yaquis, but I have seen many a peon hung out to dry after a good lashing. Forget what you might have heard about us comic-opera greasers back in Columbus, my compassionate gringo scribe. Down this way, the game is played for keeps."

CHAPTER
NINE

The Yaqui had taken only one federale alive. When they found the army truck at the end of its tire tracks, a cloud of buzzards flew up from the dozen-odd bodies they'd been feeding on. They all dismounted so the girls could hold the spooked ponies as Stringer and Villa moved in on foot to see if they could read the story.

Stringer climbed up into the cab and found the fuel gauge and water gauge read half-full. There were extra drums of water and what Villa called *gasolino* in the truck bed, along with the rifles of the motorized patrol and a couple of tin cases of extra ammo. There was no food. Villa didn't seem surprised. He said, "I see what happened. They motored past our arroyo in the dark. The Yaqui would have seen their headlamps for miles. They stopped here to have breakfast or to turn around. That is when the Yaqui hit them. The stupid bastards didn't even hold on to their guns when got out for to piss or whatever. I told you my army is better."

Stringer set the choke, made sure the gears were set right, and got out to walk around to the front of the tall beast and give the crank an experimental jerk. The engine caught on his second try. He said, "Nothing like starting warm." But Villa just looked dubious and asked, "For why are you starting the engine? I was hoping the Yaqui had lost interest in this part of the world."

"Don't be a chump," Stringer said, "This truck is watered and gassed. We can outrun any mounted Indians or, hell, cavalry, as soon as we load the girls aboard."

Villa brightened but asked, "What about the horses?" and Stringer almost said something dumb before he reconsidered and said, "Sure. Why not? We may have to blindfold 'em and have the girls hold them down on their sides. But it ought to work."

It did, after some effort. Horses just didn't like to ride trussed like calves in the back of even a big motor truck. But they quickly made up the time lost, once they got rolling. As Villa rode beside Stringer in the passenger seat, he announced that he meant to add a motor corps to his army, as soon as he could steal more army trucks from the federales. He said, "War sure has gotten interesting since I started out back in the nineties. Hey, what do you think would happen if I led a motor brigade into Columbus and taught them not to be so fresh?"

Stringer kept driving as he said, flatly, "Don't. You've already got a Mexican army to fight. How would you like the U.S. Army chasing you as well? I can promise you they will if you ever raid on our side of the border, Pancho."

Villa shrugged and muttered, "Shit. Nobody can catch me here in Chihuahua. Is rough enough country for *me* to find my way around in!"

Stringer was beginning to wonder if his would-be guide might not have a serious point by the time they'd driven a few more hours. Chihuahua seemed to just extend forever, looking much the same, until Villa, who must have had a map in his head, suggested they turn up out of the dry river bed, explaining, "Is a village ahead.

Maybe five miles. A big gringo cattle company owns the land. We'll find out when we get there who owns the people. More better we roll in unexpected, from the chaparral, no?"

So they did. It wasn't easy, and if the motor truck hadn't been rolling on solid rubber tires they'd have never made it without a flat as they crunched over several varieties of sticker-bush bearing wicked spines. Stringer was trying to navigate by the distant purple mountains that ran north to south. Villa seemed to navigate by some inner compass. So they almost wound up lost and it was pushing sunset when they finally spotted an adobe church tower ahead, almost where Villa had promised it would be. Stringer slowed down, asking, "What's the form? Don't you think it would be safer to park out here a ways and scout in afoot?"

Villa shook his head and said, "Keep going. If the people don't like us, we'll want to leave even faster. We got surprise on our side. Let's keep it that way."

So Stringer drove right into town, hoping nobody would be sophisticated enough to aim the first shot at the driver.

The villagers had obviously heard them coming. Not even a chicken was out in the open as the motor truck rolled in with its motor roaring and two ponies kicking in the back. Then Villa said, "Stop. Is not in enemy hands. Perhaps there is something to be said for absentee landlords after all, no?"

Stringer followed his gaze to where someone had scrawled, "Viva Villa" in red paint on an adobe wall. But he left the engine running, just the same, as Pancho Villa stepped out on the running board to fire a pistol in the air and bellow, "Hey, where is everybody? I am Villa! Where the fuck are you?"

Then all hell broke loose. Even the village priest rushed out of the church to greet them, though he managed to refrain from crowing like a rooster. As the joyous crowd surrounded the truck, Stringer cut the ignition, muttering, "This must be the place."

It was. Paper lanterns were lit and strung across the plaza before the sun was all the way down. Meanwhile, someone had gotten the horses out of the back, and a dozen tough looking village youths had helped themselves to the rurale rifles and lined up at attention in hopes Pancho Villa would notice them. Villa did, after he'd had some tortillas and beans washed down with pulque to show he was a man of the people. Nobody else could stand pulque. As Stringer and the girls went on eating at the trestle table erected in front of the church, Villa sort of strutted back and forth in front of the line of kids, as if deep in thought. Everyone else was jabbering away, until he stopped, put his hands on his hips, and bellowed, "*Atención!*" Then you could have cut the silence with a knife.

As the whole tiny town paid close attention, Villa intoned, "Bueno. In case you don't know yet, Los Federales just gave me a good whipping. Some of my people may have gotten away. But don't bet on it. So what have we got here? A gaggle of geese armed with guns they don't know how to use, and a whole damned federal army hot on my heels, that's what we got! You muchachos better run home to your mothers before you get hurt. Do you all want to die for nothing?"

A skinny kid with a new rifle and a ragged shirt that looked older than he was shouted back, "No! We wish for to die for Mexico!" and that inspired everyone else to yell things like "Viva Villa!" or "Kill the rich bastards!" But, after they'd begged and pleaded a while,

Villa raised a hand for silence and gruffly said, "Very well. You poor, dumb bastards get to form my honor guard. Now, I want any of you stupid cockroaches who own a gun to go get them and fall in with these heroic insects. You will probably all get killed. Even if you don't get killed, I promise you nothing but a harder life than you are already living. No uniforms. No pay. Nothing but the joy of killing other dumb bastards until we win or die!"

An old gray peon who looked too wise to talk so foolishly called out, "I have a gun. Is a muzzle loader. But it shoots straight, and any life led by a man is better than the life of a slave!"

That occasioned more yelling. As Felicidad poured tequila for Stringer she murmured, "What did I tell you? Maybe we *are* cockroaches. Maybe we are just as hard for to get *rid* of, no?"

Stringer didn't argue. Later, after his adelita had found them a place to bed down in the alcalde's house, they lay sated for the moment in each others' arms while the fiesta outside kept on going. Someone was strumming a guitar. It was almost drowned out, as boisterous voices picked up the tune to shout as much as they sang the corrido of defiant silliness, beating time with bare heels or clapping hands as they serenaded their own helplessness, or Villa's strength.

In the silence of their cozy love nest, Felicidad murmured, "You would have to be one of us to understand, Stuarto. The words must seem crazy to you, no?"

He patted her bare shoulder to reply, softly, "Not really. Once upon a time a British officer made up a silly ditty poking fun at the Yankee Militia. It caught on with us after Yankee Doodle sent Pitcairn's redcoats reeling back to Boston one long, hot April day. I guess

"La Cucaracha" ought to serve as well as a marching song, once it catches on."

Felicidad didn't answer. That last climax, coming as it did after a long, hungry day followed by all that food and drink, had apparently been too much for her. Stringer just lay there listening, until he was heartily sick of hearing about a poor ragged-ass cockroach who didn't have any marijuana, wanted some damned marijuana, and meant to just keep marching until he *got* some marijuana.

He eased the adelita's head off his naked shoulder. When she simply rolled her bare behind his way and sank deeper into the sleeping mat with a contented sigh, Stringer rolled the other way and groped on his duds, boots and gun-rig. He'd had as hard a day, but he couldn't have fallen asleep this early if his life had depended on it, and his job, if not his life, depended on him getting back to file the story before it was cold.

He knew a whole grandstand full of people, including other newspaper men, had witnessed the disastrous fight near the border. Sam Barca might forgive The *Sun* being scooped if they got to run a human interest Sunday feature on it. But not as ancient history, damn it!

He found Pancho Villa still holding court at that table set up in front of the church. Villa waved him over and said, "Sit down. They just found some gringo liquor for us. Was the property of some ranch manager who better not show up if he knows what's good for him. I just sent word to my followers on the surrounding haciendas. Nobody around here has ever followed me before. So I got to make sure I have more than enough green guns when we hit that silver mine up the river."

Stringer sat down and helped himself to some bourbon. Then he said, "Don't include me in any silver mine raids. I'm still trying to get over that battle up north. *Way* up north, and I'd just as soon not follow you any farther south, Amigo."

Villa looked sincerely puzzled as he replied, "You got to. The mine is a day's ride south. I need some money. I need the guns and dynamite they'll have there. Most important, I need a real *victory* to make up for losing that battle with Los Federales. Don't worry, I got my start raiding silver companies. The peons forced to work upstream for starvation wages won't fight us. They never do. The people here tell me there is only a small guard detachment and a few gringo mine managers. They won't be expecting us. The government just told everyone I have been killed by its brave troops, far, far away. We will cut their telegrafo wire before we move in and . . ."

"Stop right there!" Stringer cut in, explaining, "It's not my fight. I ride for the 'Frisco *Sun* and I'm paid to publish everything I know. So, do you really want to let me in on how you mean to rob an international trust's silver mine, Pancho?"

Villa looked just as innocent as he answered, "Sure. I told you I liked you because you told the truth about me. I want you to report my victory just as it happens. By the time anyone on the others side can read your newspaper, me and my army won't be anywhere near the gringo silver mine. I just want it known that I am not a cowardly bandit who shoots pigs and chickens and runs away from men. So listen, here is my plan . . ."

"Damn it, Pancho," Stringer cut in again, "I just told you I can't afford to spend any more time down here with you. If I thought my tagging along would make a difference I might be willing to lose my job *Por Mejico*

Libre. But it won't. So it's time I headed back and . . .
about that army truck . . ."

"I need it," said Villa, flatly, adding, "Is part of my
plan. There are always two-faced ones in every village
who hope to better their lives by carrying tales to the
other side. So we got to get up to that mine faster than a
raton can push his caballo. Is plenty room in the back
for the few soldados I picked up here. Maybe I can
recruit some more closer to the mine. Either way, it will
be close and I need surprise on my side, see?"

Stringer tried, "Okay, if you're taking the truck you
ought to be able to spare me a pony. Just one lousy pony
and maybe four canteens?"

Villa shook his head gravely and said, "No. I like
you too much to let the Yaqui have you. You would
never make it on your own. Besides, I need you to drive
the motor truck. I don't know how. These others here,
can barely ride a horse."

Stringer swore, Stringer pleaded, he even tried to get
Villa drunk. But the stocky Mex was adamant, too intent on the big win he needed to feel the effects of mere
booze, or even wed the alcalde's daughter this time.
When Stringer asked him about the girls they'd already
married, Villa shrugged and told him, "They'll catch up
in time, if we win. If we lose, they'll find some other
band to follow. I have enough trouble moving my *men*
around. Is the duty of an adelita to get there the best
way she can. Do not pester me about pussy when I am
planning more serious matters, you gringo Don Juan.
When a man is winning, he has no need for to look for
women. They flock to winners as the tumbleweed piles
against the fence. Is only the losers who have to jerk
themselves off. You will see, if you ride with me just a
little further. After we improve our fortunes at that

silver mine, you shall be free to ride home in style. There is a railroad from the silver smelters to the main line. After we finish plundering the place, I mean to load my army aboard the company train and strike at Durango next. Nobody will expect us to hit that far south, and they got lots of nice banks in Durango. But you can catch a train north to El Paso if you don't want to watch us rob banks. We won't rob any trains until you are safely on your way. I told you I liked you."

Stringer didn't answer. He left the rest of his booze right where it was and got up to find a private place to ponder. There had to be a better way to get back to the states. He dismissed a heap of notions as he sat on the church steps away from the crowd, rolling Bull Durham as much to keep his hands from shaking than from any real desire to smoke. Stealing a horse would be easy enough, he knew, and he doubted Villa would follow him. But the federale the Yaqui had worked over had sure looked miserable. Stringer idly wondered if he was dead by now. How long could a guy last, and how far could he wander, with the soles of his feet peeled off like that, even if he could still see?

Stringer knew the Mex authorities wouldn't treat him a whole lot better if they caught him robbing silver mines with outlaws. For, bandit or liberator, Villa was an outlaw to the Diaz regime. One of the nicer ways Mex lawmen treated outlaws was by forcing them to dig their own graves, gut-shooting them, and burying them alive. That might not smart as much as being tortured by Yaqui, but it wasn't anything Stringer really wanted to experience first hand. He finally finished rolling his smoke, and as he struck a match on the stone steps to light it muttered, "I don't see why Villa's being so optimistic. We're sure to get mowed down by the company guns if we hit a mine in bandit country with a lousy handful of green kids!"

Then things got worse. Everyone stopped singing "La Cucaracha" as the sounds of a familiar gas buggy approached from the north, tingling the night air as, again, someone insisted on driving that poor Maxwell full-choke in low gear. Stringer had set it full choke in neutral when he'd parked it out front of Villa's tent that time, a time that now seemed long ago indeed. He got up and tagged along as everyone flocked to admire the second motor vehicle most of them had ever seen in their backward lives. As the Maxwell, beige as the army truck now, its black factory finish coated with desert dust, pulled into the square and stopped with a tinny gargle and a backfire, Villa strode over to shake with his segundo, Hernan. They were both grinning like kids who'd been swiping apples. Villa cocked an eyebrow at the eleven dusty soldados crowded into the five passenger touring car to demand, "How the hell did you muchachos make it? Didn't they hit our camp?"

Hernan climbed out stiffly, saying, "With artillery, too. I think they were lobbing 105s. They really tore the shit out of things. Was a very cruel way to treat women and horses. But, as you see, this tin caballo is tough. After dark, we crept back to push it back up on its wheels and so here we are, My General. I don't know how many others made it. These are all I could find in the dark."

Stringer drifted over to join them. If he could persuade Villa to part with just that Maxwell and a full tank . . .

But he couldn't. Villa waved him closer, grinning ear to ear as he chortled, "Now we are back in business. We got two gasolino wagons to carry almost a full platoon into battle and at least half you muchachos can hit the side of the granero as long as you stand inside it. Listen, Hernan, I just got a new plan. We shall move like the wind up the river, so we can hit the mining settlement from two sides at once before they know we are anywhere near them. Maybe I plan a diversion. Do any of you from the camp have any nail bombs left?"

Hernan shrugged and said, "Sure. We got a sack of them in the back. In God's truth, they still throw more smoke than nails, though. I saw one of our pobrecitos toss one right at a federale rider and the bastard just rode through the ball of smoke and sabered him."

Villa grinned and said, "Is not important. We just need lots of noise and smoke. Stringer, here, will be in command of that detail."

Stringer started to argue, then just sighed and said, "Why not? The sooner I can get you loco bastards out of my hair the better. So let's get it over with."

Stringer hoped they'd strike at dawn. He'd punched the army truck south through the chaparral to the east of the dry river bed, driving with the headlamps extinguished and hoping Villa, in the passenger seat, knew where the hell they were. Hernan was supposed to be driving south on the far side, if the gears of the abused Maxwell held out. Stringer had tried to show the segundo how to shift gears before they'd left that village. But Hernan was an independent thinker.

Most of Villa's new "army", green or seasoned, was naturally with Stringer and Villa. Hernan's four sharpshooters were picked for that detail because they didn't have to stand inside a barn to hit it broadside, if that was what Hernan wanted them to hit. Stringer was still slightly vague on the overall plan. Villa and Hernan had ridden together long enough to savvy each other's intentions without having to discuss things all that much. Villa filled Stringer in better during the long desert drive. Stringer was glad he and the two kids assigned to him weren't being asked to kill anyone.

Of course, if the others messed up, that'd leave him and two scared peons in a swell position, on foot in the chaparral against an outfit too tough for the deadly Villa. But as the sky began to pearl the starry sky to the east, Stringer consoled himself with the thought that they were, most likely, lost. _

Then Villa, one booted foot out on the running board to the west, snapped, "Aqui! We made it! Stop the engine before we wake up the soon-to-be-dead!"

Switching off the ignition was no problem. Stringer still couldn't see anything interesting in the dim light surrounding them. Then he, too, heard the babble of running water, or at least a mighty leaky tap. As Villa dropped to the ground and headed for the soft wet sounds, Stringer followed after. It was a short scout to the east bank of the dry river. It was only dry to the north. A flat expanse of shiny India ink reflected the stars above as far upstream as they could see, which was less than a few hundred yards, but still added up to a hell of a lot of imprisoned water. There wasn't enough of a head to the long, low dam built across the river bed to worry about hydraulic power. The silver company had simply dammed the stream to hog such water as there was for its steam engines and such, out of sight upstream in this light. The water they'd heard running was pouring through a rusty floodgate on their side of the dam. It probably wasn't supposed to be running at all. But they had plenty more upstream and the few gallons a minute they were losing couldn't amount to the loss to evaporation when the Chihuahua sun was up. The rivulet from the leaky floodgate just soaked into the dry river bed before it could do anyone or anything any good. Villa said, "Bueno. You stay here. I'll send in the muchachos with the sack of bombs before I lead the others up to the mine on foot. Don't do anything until you hear Hernan open up from the high ground on the far side. Then make all the noise you can down here to convince them this dam is the main objective. The farmers downstream have been complaining about this dam ever since the silver company built it. Some of the company guards will rush down here to save the dam. Others will be trading shots with Hernan's detail, expecting to be rushed, if they get rushed at all, by wild men from the hills. That is when me and the main force will charge in from the open desert and . . ."

"You call that truck load of guys a main force?" Stringer cut in, adding, "Pancho, you're taking too much of a chance. They're sure to have all approaches covered, stuck as they are out here in the middle of nowhere."

But Villa insisted, "That is why I am a general and they are not. Sure they'll have what they consider their weaker points covered. But both bandits and Yaqui like to charge downhill and does not that shitty floodgate tell you they are a cheap? The owners live far away, on your street of walls. They don't give a shit for anyone down here, as long as the mine makes a profit. I could tell you tales of absentee owners who would rather see a child torn up by their mill machinery than pay for a guard rail, or, hell, hire someone old enough to watch what she was doing. But right now I have to take them out, not talk about them. So *hasta la vista* and try not to fuck up."

Then he was gone. Stringer hunkered down on his spurred bootheels and thoughtfully began to roll a smoke as, somewhere in the night, a borrowing owl called his name. That was what the Miwok back home said owls were calling when you were up to something dumb as hell in the dark. Like most Indians, the Miwok considered the owl the totem of Old Woman, or Death. She sent owls out to gather the spirits. Everybody had four spirits and at least one went to live with Old Woman in her lodge, somewhere up north. The northern lights were the glow from Old Woman's lodge fire, when she left her smoke ears open to sing with all her spirit guests.

He licked the gummed seal of his rolled smoke and lit it, shielding the flame with his cupped palms against the eyes of Owl, or anyone else out there who might be interested. Having one of his four spirits picked up by Owl seemed easy enough at the rate things were going. Even the Indians seemed confused about the three spirits left over. It was sort of like getting a sensible explanation of The Trinity from a sky pilot. He still recalled how Crazy Aunt Ida had fussed at him for bringing that note home from Sunday school that time. In the end, Uncle Don had saved him from a licking. Uncle Don had said he'd never entirely savvied the point of The Trinity, and allowed that even in Gaelic that story about shamrocks didn't prove anything save for the fact that some weeds had three leaves. Crazy Aunt Ida had insisted it was *supposed* to be a mystery and that they'd end up in Hades, she never said Hell, if they didn't both just *hush*!

The two kids from the village came to join him. Now that they had gun belts crossed on their skinny chests they still just looked like kids to Stringer. One had the feed sack of grenades. As the two of them hunkered down by Stringer, the one carrying the sack asked where to set them if they wanted to blow the dam.

Stringer said, "I've been wondering about that, myself. That earthfill dam looks pretty solid. Those cannisters offer more sound than fury. You could play hell with a man's hide if you set one off anywheres near him. But I doubt they'd dig a footdeep hole in soft ground and that dam's tamped clay with a tar facing."

One of the kids said, "The great Pancho Villa said he is counting on us to blow that dam, no?" To which Stringer replied, "No. He wants us to make the guards upstream think that's what we're doing. The noise ought to carry. We can make swell clouds down here if we bury them under piles of fine dust before we light the fuses. So that's how we'd better begin."

They did. Neither farm boy argued as they piled all the grenades in one spot on the higher ground just east of the dam and scooped double handfuls of dust over them. Anyone could see the results would be a mighty pillar of smoke and dust against the morning sky, if morning ever got here. But when they asked him again what damage all this might do to the dam, Stringer said only, "Let's see," and moved over to the floodgate.

Despite the way it was leaking, the big rusty plate didn't want to budge when Stringer tried turning the wheel crank to lift it. He said, "Shit," and told them to help. With all three of them straining, the gate stayed as if it had been welded shut. "Harder," he grunted, "All together," and suddenly something snapped and he gasped, "Basta!" as water began to run indeed. It was almost as hard to crank the floodgate shut again and once they had, anyone could see it was leaking worse, now. He grimaced and said, "We may have started something. So what could be keeping Hernan? It's getting lighter by the minute."

All three of them could see the rocky slopes to the west of the river had turned blood red against the still-dark sky over that way. Stringer turned the other way to see the distant army truck outlined against the pearly dawn. That was something to think about. But the gas gauges read low, now, and he'd have to kill these two young boys to get enough of a lead to matter, now that the others had that Maxwell to track him with if he messed up Villa's plan.

But, what was going wrong with Villa's plan? The time for a sunrise attack was right about now, with the sun in the eyes of the attackees. As if to prove him right, the sun came up making his eyes water as he tried to make out details against its hot, angry stare. "There's never going to be a better time for Villa to make his move," he muttered, "Something's gone wrong!"

Then something went wrong in a big way. It sounded like God kicking one hell of a bucket when the floodgate, further weakened by their tampering, gave way all at once to let the imprisoned water go anywhere it wanted with a deep-throated roar.

"Oh, shit, back to the truck, pronto!" as he hunkered to light the exposed fuse of his ammunition pile with his cigarette. Then he was off and running, too. But when he got to the army truck, he saw only one of the kids had beaten him there. He turned to see the other, watching by the bank in fascination as the white water arced out at express train speed to dig itself a pot hole downstream. Stringer yelled and, when that didn't work, he drew his .38 and fired in the air. The distant kid turned with a curious smile. Then the pile of grenades went off less than ten feet from him, and he wasn't there anymore.

The explosion sent a huge mustard colored mushroom skyward, turning a dirty shade of dusty rose as the sun hit it higher up. The kid next to Stringer gasped, "*Ay carramba*! I bet they can see that in *Ciudad Mejico*! *Pero*, what has become of Ramon?"

Stringer sighed and said, "Welcome to the club. A good *soldado* takes orders. Ramon didn't. So now he's what we call a casualty. It sounds nicer than blown to shit. Get in the cab. It's time to put some distance between ourselves and that distraction. If it worked, we ought to have a lot of distracted company down this way, *poco tiempo*."

That was easier said than done. When Stringer cranked the big four banger engine, it just coughed and tried to bust his arm with the kickback. He checked the gas gauge again. Low as it read, it seemed over-optimistic. He told the bewildered young Mex, "We have to run for it, Vamanos!"

They ran for it, straight at the sunrise at first, both to get away from the river, and to make themselves tougher to aim at. Then Stringer heard the crackle of small arms fire to their right and grunted, "Lesson numero dos: when in doubt, move on the sound of the guns" and headed in that direction.

The kid gasping in his wake demanded to know why, panting, "It sounds like a big fight that way, no?"

Stringer answered, "Safety in numbers. Alone out

here, we're dead meat. Are you any good with that military rifle?"

The kid said he didn't know. He hadn't fired it yet. Stringer swore softly and took it from him, saying soothingly, "Don't look so sad. You can carry the ammo, see?"

The light was a lot better now. They could see more smoke rising above sunlit tin roofing and a tall smelter stack as they waded south through waist-high chaparral. After that, it was up for grabs. They could hear guns going off, a lot of guns going off, but they couldn't tell who was winning, or even where everybody was. Then the kid gasped, "Behind us!" and Stringer dove headfirst to land on one shoulder and roll with the rifle held across his chest, as another rifle squibbed in the distance. Stringer got behind a clump of creosote bush and worked the bolt of the army rifle as he rose on one knee for a look-see. The kid he'd been with was down out of sight. A trio of riders were coming his way from the north. They reined in when they spotted his hat to take better aim. Stringer knew the one with the rifle was the one he had to worry about the most, so he spilled him first. Then he got one of the pistol hands as they quickly lost interest in him. The last survivor came closer to making it as he streaked away to the north, crouched low over the horn. But Stringer took careful aim and put a .30-06 slug up his ass, or close enough to the actual point of aim to lift him out of his saddle and somersault him out of sight. Then Stringer muttered, "That's better. Hey, Tomas? Come out come out wherever you are."

There was no answer. He found the kid less than fifty feet away, face up, with a shy little smile on his face and a little blue hole in his forehead. Stringer muttered, "You're supposed to hit the dirt, not just *stand* there."

Then he stripped the thin corpse of its ammo belts and strapped them across his own chest, muttering, "Viva Villa, you poor skinny little idiot."

Then he pressed on to see who'd won, knowing he was in deep shit if Villa had lost again.

CHAPTER
TEN

But this time Villa had won. It hadn't been easy. He'd lost four men, or boys, from that village, hitting the mining layout from the east when the diversionary explosion to the north and falling water had given him little other choice. As Stringer joined Villa and his tiny army on the veranda of the manager's combined office and quarters, Villa said he didn't know what had happened to Hernan, either. But he waved expansively at the few bodies sprawled out front to add, "Was easier than we had the right to hope for. Was only a handful of gringo supervisors here. The armed guards are in my army, now. Was stupid to hire Mexicans of my class as guards, no?"

Stringer suggested, "Maybe they were trying to save money. I'm sorry I went off early like that. I had to when I saw the water was going down on its own. I lost those two kids. I shot three company men. They looked Anglo to me."

Villa nodded and said, "Bueno. The one captive we took alive says the manager and a couple of assistants got away by running for it. They must have worked in Mexico a while. We just blew the safe, so now we have a war chest and the fourteen armed guards and their rifles will more than make up our losses, even if we've lost Hernan and his sharpshooters. What do you think might have happened to them? Is nothing but Yaqui over that way."

Stringer said, "You might have just answered your own question. Hadn't we ought to think about getting the hell out of here, now?"

Villa shook his head. He said, "Not yet. We got to wait for Hernan. It will take Los Federales at least a full day and night to decided what to do, even if they know what we have done here. No federale is going to risk his fancy ass before he knows just what he might be up against. By now, word is spreading far and wide that Villa rides again! Maybe we wait here a few days and see how many flock to join us, no?"

"I've got a better idea. Why don't you just shove a gun up your nose and pull the trigger? You can't make a stand here, Pancho. You just took the place with a handful of men and there's no line of retreat if those hills to the west are infested with Yaqui!"

Villa shrugged and said, "I don't like to retreat in any case. It gives a general a bad name and I've already been whipped once this week. Do you know how to work a telegrafo? We did not have time to cut the wire, as I'd planned. Is a set inside. I would like to know what the world is saying about me right now."

Stringer said he'd try, so Villa led the way into the main office, where the floor was littered with papers and a blond girl in a dirty white uniform was kneeling by the open safe trying to do something about the shattered head of an elderly Anglo gent even Stringer could see was beyond medical help. Villa waved at the wide-eyed girl and explained, "She is the live captive I mentioned. Maybe later, I marry her. She's got lots of guts. We found her here, trying to help that old man, when she could have gotten away with the others."

Stringer knew they were talking about some length of time by now. If the girl really was a nurse, she'd had plenty of time to notice her patient was dead. Stringer switched to English to say, "You've done all you can for him, Miss." But she just stared back, wide-eyed. He nodded to himself and told Villa in Spanish, "She's in a state of shock. I don't think she wants to marry anybody. That could be one of the things that's bothering her, right now. Would you mind if I sort of took her under my wing?"

Villa said, "Go ahead and screw her, if you like her looks. We'll have mucho adelitas flocking in, now. But, first, see what they are saying about me on the telegrafo, eh?"

Stringer moved over to the telegraph set on a heavy desk that could have been the manager's, before he'd been let go without notice. Stringer sat behind the desk and tapped out a C.Q. There was no reply. He told Villa, "If anyone's home at the far end, they don't want to talk to us. Assuming the line's still open, the hombres who used to work here got off a last message before they lit out."

Villa asked, "Can you signal that I wish Diaz to know I think he would fuck his mother if she was not so ugly?"

Stringer chuckled dryly and said, "I doubt they'd relay that message to him in so many words. Why tell them we're still here? Why not let them think we hit and ran?"

Villa nodded and said, "Bueno. Tell them I am on my way to the capital to flush Diaz down his fancy toilet. Tell them that I, Villa, am marching south at the head of a mighty army!"

Stringer sent the message. If it did nothing else, it might confuse them over near the main line. That reminded Stringer of what Villa had said earlier about the company tracks. But when he asked about that, Villa looked disgusted and said, "Is no locomotive here. Maybe that is how they got away. Or maybe the company train left with some silver before we got here. Let us ask this woman they left behind."

Stringer tried talking to her in English. The girl just went on staring down at the dead man she was kneeling over until he gently touched her shoulder. Then she sobbed, "Don't hurt me! I'm a nurse. I wasn't shooting at anyone and, oh, whatever shall I do for poor Mister Teasdale?"

Stringer tried, "He's dead, miss." But that just made her shake her head and sob, "Oh, no, he can't be. I won't let it be. I have to make him better."

Stringer looked at Villa and tapped his own temple with a finger. Villa nodded and said, "*Loco en la cabeza.* You're sure you want her? Not much fun to screw a lunatic, even a pretty one, and my own sainted mamacita told us lunacy was catching."

Stringer didn't answer. He knew most Indians were afraid to mess with the insane and Villa admitted to Chihuahua blood. He gently but firmly hauled the petite blond to her feet. The knees of her white skirt were sticky with blood.

"We want to get you cleaned up and calmed down, Miss. Where are your quarters?"

She murmured, "Down at the end of the veranda. Please don't hurt me. I've never been bad to your people."

Stringer exchanged glances with Villa, who nodded but said, "Is a little early, if you ask me. Why not wait and see what may turn up? That one could use some meat on her bones as well as some brains in her head."

Stringer said he'd be back too soon for anyone to worry about his virtue and led the quivering little nurse out on the veranda. The open space out front had been left to the morning sun and the sprawled bodies. A veteran of the battle to the north was lounging in the shade with a heavily-armed local recruit. As Stringer led the girl past them, the soldado who knew him grinned to say, "Oh, you Yanquis! May we claim sloppy seconds?"

Stringer assumed the one who knew him was just kidding. The recent company guard sounded more ominous as he growled, "Hey, how come the gringo gets that stuck-up little bitch? We have feelings, too, and I've always wanted some of that."

Stringer left them to debate the matter as he got the blonde to cover, *poco tiempo*. Her corner room had cross ventilation and a big brass bedstead occupied at the moment by a too-cute rag doll with flirty eyes. He locked the door behind them and did a little exploring. There was an adjoining bath, with shower, and some darker dresses hung in a big oaken wardrobe across from the bed. The girl hadn't moved from the center of the floor since he'd led her in. He joined her there, saying, "Snap out of it. You're safe, for now. You'd better take a quick shower, put on the darkest dress you own, and cover your hair with a mantilla or at least a kerchief. You'll be safer if we can get you to sort of blend in, see?"

She stared at him with eyes that were beginning to focus a little better as it sank in that he was instructing her in English. She licked her pale lips and asked, "What are you doing with these greaser bandits if you're American, like me?"

"Pancho Villa doesn't consider himself a bandit, and I don't think you'd better call him a greaser to his face. I was just about to ask you what you were doing on the other side. If I had my druthers, neither one of us would be down here. It's not our fight."

She said, "I didn't come down here to fight anyone. I was sent by the company as an angel of mercy, only they refuse to send the supplies I ordered, and I fear most of the emergencies I've had to cope with would be beyond the skills of most graduates of the Harvard Medical School. It makes you feel so dumb and helpless when all you can do for an injured miner is hold his hand until he passes away. They hate me here. They think I don't care when they get hurt or sick."

He nodded and said, "I'll pass the word it was company policy. What nursing school in the States might you be a graduate of?"

She looked away. He smiled thinly and said, "Right. Why hire a real R.N. when you can just go through the motions and save a heap of dinero? For real, miss, who and what are you?"

Her eyes got misty again as she almost whispered, "My name is Roberta Davis. My friends call me Bobbie. I'm the widow of a mining engineer who died in a cave-in two years ago. The company was kind enough to find me this position on their payroll, so . . ."

"So they saved themselves the widow's pension and even a ticket back to the states." He cut in, too polite to add that she seemed pretty dumb even when she wasn't hysterical. Hoping she'd calmed down enough to pay attention, he told her, "I have to get back on the job, Bobbie. I want you to lock the door after me and stay put. Remember what I said about changing out of that uniform and getting your blond hair under cover. I'll get back to you when Villa makes up his mind about moving on, or, failing that, I'll be back at siesta time with some food and drink. Can you last that long just on tap water?"

She said she had too many butterflies in her stomache to drink even water, and begged him not to leave her alone, lest some rude greaser subject her to a fate worse than death. He told her, "I can't think of a fate worse than death. Nobody will mess with you once I spread the word that you're my adelita, with the full approval of Pancho Villa."

She blushed like a rose and turned her back to him as she flustered, "I guess I have no other choice, but you will try to be gentle, won't you? It's been some times since I've . . . You know, and this has all been so sudden!"

He chuckled and assured her, "I meant in name only. You have to understand that Hispanic women are treated with the respect due the man who claims the right to defend their honor. Without at least a tough brother to stick up for her, the Virgin Mary would be up for grabs. My name's MacKail, Stuart MacKail. Remember that and feel free to invoke it should anybody try to mess with you. Don't struggle. It's not considered womanly. Just bat your lashes and say you'd just love to kiss such a handsome gent but that your hombre, that's me, might be jealous."

She told him she wasn't sure she could be that subtle, given her limited grasp of Spanish. He told her to start learning the lingo and meanwhile do the best she knew how.

Then he ducked out before she could ask more dumb questions.

He knew he had enough on his own plate and that

this was no time to play Sir Galahad. But he knew he couldn't just leave her to be passed around as a play pretty, as she would, if he just left her behind when he got his own chance to make a break for it. Villa himself was okay. But it was no secret that most of his mestizo followers hated Americans, sometimes with good reason. If Bobbie spoke no Spanish and hadn't really been much of a nurse, they no doubt had her down as just another stuck-up member of the ruling class. He'd interviewed old-timers of the G.A.R. and knew that while it hadn't gotten into the history books, Sherman's march through Georgia had been tough on many a southern belle once the liberated field hands had waved adios to the boys in blue. Folk who kept others in slavery never seemed to learn, until too late, that a grinning and fawning bond servant could store up one hell of a lot of resentment as even an easygoing master got to laze about sipping juleps. And, as always in times of sudden change, it seemed to be the more innocent members of the ruling class that suffered most. The really mean bastards got to the lifeboats first. Diaz would probably retire in a few years as he said. A lot of other grandees had Swiss bank accounts and carried steamer tickets in their wallets. It was the smaller landlords and officers of lower rank that figured to wind up against the wall in the end.

Stringer went back to where he'd left Villa, but nobody was in the office now. They'd even hauled the dead Anglo out. When Stringer glanced out the window, he saw the bodies out front had been cleared away as well. A quartet of Mex women were turning an ox, or perhaps a burro, over the fire pit they'd just put in business. Stringer went out to join them, in hopes they had some idea what was going on. The girl turning the spit was sort of pretty, despite the wood ash on her brown face. She told him the meat was still raw, inside. He said he could wait for *La Fiesta* to start officially and asked where the four of them might have come from. An older and fatter woman explained, "We are with the army of liberation, now. This morning we were only the mujeres of peon mine workers. Now we march as ade-litas with Pancho Villa. You can ask him if you do not believe us!"

Stringer said he felt sure they had Villa's blessings and added, "We live in times of change. I would like it known that La Señora Davis, who used to be the com-pany nurse, will be marching as my adelita, now."

The pretty one scowled and demanded, "For why? Just because she has frog-belly skin and yellow hair? Hey, I got some hair to show you, Americano. That gringa has no fire between her legs. You will see."

Stringer laughed and told her she was wrong. It wasn't gallant to talk that way about a gal, even when you'd really had her. But this was not a gallant situation and he wanted them to gossip dirty about him and Bob-bie. So, knowing they surely would, he moved on.

There was a water tower near the railroad trestle Villa and his boys had charged across earlier, as the water under it went down. This far up from the dam, the stream bed was now a sea of chocolate mud, already starting to crust and crack under the Chihuahua sun. Down closer to the dam there was, no doubt, quite a swimming hole left. The open floodgate could have only let so much water out.

Stringer started climbing the ladder of the water tower with his captured army rifle slung across his back. It was all very well for the guerrillas to take such a casual attitude toward the basic rules of organised warfare, but he wanted some idea just what the hell was going on.

When he got to the platform the big redwood tank rested on, Stringer learned Pancho Villa was not as half-assed as he'd feared. One of the recruits from the village was posted up there with a pair of field glasses. He helped Stringer up the last few rungs and asked if he'd been relieved at last.

"I'm afraid you're still pulling look-out," Stringer replied, "Call this an inspection. Have you seen anything worth reporting, yet?"

The kid shrugged and said, "Sunshine and buzzards. Is too hot now to make out movement on the horizon."

Stringer followed his gaze to the east, across the shimmering desert. It wasn't that one couldn't see movement out there. The whole scene was moving as if reflected in a disturbed millpond. He followed the twin ribbons of sun-baked steel extending from near the base of the tower to an uncertain vanishing point. The railroad line seemed to be twisting like a skinny steel snake as it slithered off to the east through the chaparral. A dirt service road and a string of dancing telegraph poles shimmered out of step with the single track rail line. He told the kid, "A train coming our way would be moving under a smudge of coal smoke long before you could make out movement on the ground." The boy replied that Villa had already told him to watch for smoke.

Stringer moved around the platform for a bird's-eye view of the mining complex itself. From a defensive standpoint, he didn't like what he saw. The main building with its wraparound veranda stood close to the smelter up the tracks, where they ended. There was a stamping mill and piles of silver ore and coal. That part seemed compact enough to fortify with earthworks strung from strong point to strong point, but after that, things commenced to sprawl. The adobe and brush one-roomers of the mine workers lay mostly to the south, scattered helter skelter as the people had just thrown them up in their spare time wherever they'd felt like it. Villa didn't have the forces to dig in that far out, and the damned shacks still provided lots of cover for skirmishers moving in. Any federale officer with the brains of a gnat and a survey chart of the area would stop his troop train well out on the desert and have his men move in to pay house calls as they leapfrogged in.

Stringer moved around to the west side as the kid drifted along, trying to be helpful. It was easier to judge the distance to the barren hills to the west from up here. They were, in fact, further away than they looked from ground level. Way the hell out of rifle range. So that might account for Hernan's failure to follow that part of the plan, though it didn't account for where the devil Hernan and his sharp shooters might be at *this* late date. Stringer had a clear view of the mine entrance and the narrow-gauge tram line leading from the mine to the refining layout. He knew the miners had been expected to push the heavy ore trams the hard way, barefoot. He asked the kid with him just how many of the locals had joined up. The kid shrugged and said, "Most of the guards, maybe half the miners, and all their women, of course. I make it fifty or sixty men and about a hundred adelitas, now. A nice big army, no?"

Stringer didn't answer. Felicidad had told him why peon women were ever anxious to exchange a life of cruel drudgery for a life on the owlhoot trail. They expected only to screw a lot more and grind corn meal a lot less. Men didn't like to join armies unless they could carry a gun. So Villa would have to do something about his ordnance problem before he could recruit more men to tag along. Stringer asked what they'd done about the mine workers who'd refused to join. The kid shrugged and said, "Nothing. They have nothing. Why waste ammunition on cowards? Perhaps they hope to someday work here again. Even bad jobs are hard to come by in this country. Pancho says not to hurt anyone who does not get in our way. Some of them seem put out by the loss of their women. But, what is a man who has no gun and no will to fight the government to do? We are twice as tough as the government, you know."

Stringer had certain reservations about that. Both the regular army and Los Rurales, who combined the duties of the Texas Rangers and U.S. marshals, had been fighting rebels, and winning, long before most of Villa's current band had been born. But it wasn't his problem.

They moved around to the north side. All too aware of how far over the shimmering horizon the border was, Stringer saw what the kid had meant about buzzards. Those three bodies out by the stalled army truck had sure attracted a flock of them. From the way they still circled, it seemed at least one of the meals he'd left out there for them was still breathing. Stringer gulped down the green taste in his mouth as he thought about how long it had been. He was sure young Tomas had been dead for hours. If one of the other three was still waving off buzzards, it was just tough titty. It had been their notion to fire first, and he knew they'd have left him in the same fix if they'd won.

Due north, he saw he'd been right about the dam. The water had only dropped five or six feet. Some tiny tawny figures seemed to be skinny-dipping in the shallow lake it created. He told the kid he'd been wondering where everyone had gone. The kid sighed wistfully and replied, "I wish it was me down there. I don't know what gets into women, once they decide to march in the manner of adelitas. I'll bet you last night a lot of them were lighting candles to the saints lest their husbands beat them for suffering yet another headache after a long hot day at their looms or earthen stoves. Now they are behaving as naked pagan girls, and enjoying every momento as they frolic with their new lovers. I wonder if it's true we're going to shoot all the priests but just the ugly nuns when we get our country back?"

Stringer cautiously replied that he hadn't heard Villa was at war with the Mexican church.

The kid shrugged and said "Pancho says it is wrong to loot churches. But Los Colorados and some of the other rebel bands are not as superstitious. They say the priests work hand in glove with the grandees, getting fat and rich as they tell ignorant people they will burn in Hell if they fail to obey their masters. They got lots of gold, whole altars of gold, in lots of churches. Pancho says after he becomes El Presidente, he can make all the money the people need with just a printing press. But I don't know. The man who runs the cantina in my village says paper money is no good unless you got some gold to back it up, and the priests got lots of gold."

Stringer tried to change the subject. He'd never been able to talk much sense to folk who could *read* Marx and Engels' drivel. He knew the most bloodthirsty Marxists were the ones who'd only memorized a few slogans and didn't know that Karl Marx had lived pretty high on the hog with a staff of house servants. He pointed out a distant smudge of rising dust, far to the northwest, between the river and the hills, saying, "That looks like one rider or maybe a handful of men on foot. Maybe Yaqui?"

The kid stared soberly for a time before he decided, "Yaqui don't move out that far from the hills in daylight. Whatever it is, it's moving too slow for a rider. We better tell Pancho, I think."

Stringer said, "I'll tell him. I was looking for him to begin with. Do you know where he might be right now?"

The kid pointed to the distant brown dots splashing around by the dam and said, "Sure. Swimming. You got to grow up in Chihuahua to know how good it feels for to splash in water when you get the chance. He likes naked women, too."

Stringer climbed back down the ladder laughing, and strode north along the bank. The swimming hole was farther away than it looked. The sun was hot and he was sweating in his none too clean blue denims long before he got close enough to hear Pancho Villa call out, boisterously, "Hey, Stringer, come on in. The water's fine!"

The bevy of brown skinned beauties splashing about with the burly Villa looked fine, too. Even saggy tits looked swell when they were supported by water. Stringer started to object. But he had to get to the west bank, anyway. So he hauled off his jacket and gun rig to carry his possibles above his head with the rifle as he waded out, boots and all. The water was warm as stale tea, thanks to the desert sun. But it felt good as it rose to his armpits. He joined Villa and the bathing beauties to say, "There's something coming in from the northwest. Looks like a small party. But I thought you'd like to know."

Villa nodded, told the girls to climb out the far side and take cover, then called out to some of his male swimming partners and said, "Let's go. We left our stuff on the west bank with just such surprises in mind."

So they all waded across. As Villa and the others climbed the clay bank bare-assed naked, Stringer tossed his rifle and possibles ashore and ducked all the way under, coming up to spout water like a whale and mutter, "That's better. My stubble will just have to wait."

It only took Villa and his four followers a few moments to look armed and dangerous again. Villa motioned everyone to spread out as they fanned away from the river. When Villa hunkered down behind a clump of prickly pear, Stringer took cover behind a mesquite and worked the bolt of his rifle. A million years went by. Then Villa muttered, "Bueno, it's about time!"

Then he rose to wave his hat, calling out, "Hernan! Over here! Where in the name of all the saints have you been?"

As the very dusty and disgusted-looking Hernan came on in with his worn-out sharpshooters, he called back, "That damned gringo motor car blew up. We thought Los Federales had dropped a shell on us. But was only the engine. We've been walking all night and for hours since sunrise. I hope we got here in time for the fun."

Villa laughed and said, "Was lots of fun, and now we're going to have a fiesta. Only first we have to take a siesta. Is getting hot as the hinges of hell, no?"

The husky Hernan licked his dusty lips and said, "We had not noticed. Is that *water* I see shining through the brush behind you?"

Villa said it sure was and added, "Feel free to jump in and cool off. Then we better go back upstream and rest in the shade. We got it all thanks to Stringer, here."

The sharpshooters Hernan had led this far were already on their way to the swimming hole, but Hernan stared thoughtfully at Stringer as he asked, "What did this gringo do that was so wonderful? I thought we'd agreed I was to fire the opening shots. How come you did not wait for us, Pancho?"

Villa snorted, "You'd better cool your head. The sun has fried your brains. We agreed the attack was to be at dawn. It is now closer to noon. You were not here to start anything, so Stringer made lots of noise down here by the dam and I led the others in from the east as planned. Was a nice little fight. It all went smooth as silk, even if you missed it."

Hernan knew better than to glare at Villa, so he glared at Stringer instead as he complained, "I see it all, now. To get in good with you, this gringo did something to that Maxwell's motor to make it blow up. It was *my* job to create a diversion, not his!"

Gently but firmly Villa said, "Go soak your head, muchacho. Stringer tried to show you how to drive that motor car. You did not listen. Was your own fault you got left behind. Stringer did a good job when you failed to do your part and I do not wish to argue about it. Cool your fevered brain. Enjoy a nice siesta. Then we'll all feel better, no?"

Hernan growled deep in his throat, so Stringer was able to pretend he didn't hear that part about his mother as the husky Hernan bulled his way through the chaparral toward the swimming hole.

Villa turned to Stringer and sighed, "I am glad you decided not to hear that. I like you both. Hernan is not usually so sullen. Let us hope it is over between you, eh?"

Stringer shrugged and said, "I was brought up to turn

the other cheek and then kill the bastard if he slapped *that* one. So, what if it's *not* over?"

"I just said I hoped it was. I can stop him if he challenges you. If he starts to play "Tu Madre" with you, well, you are on your own, as long as it's a fair fight. I got to maintain *some* discipline, damn it."

So there it was, like a gobbet of spit on the card table, and Stringer knew how "Tu Madre" was played. He knew he'd be in deep shit whether he won or lost. So he could only hope Hernan would cool down. There was nothing anyone else could do but wait and see.

By the time Stringer rejoined Bobbie Davis in her quarters with the canned provisions and jug of rum he'd salvaged, his duds were dry and his socks were getting there. Nobody who'd spent more than a day in Mexico had to have the almost sacred ritual of La Siesta explained. But the American girl wasn't up on the even older custom of "Tu Madre," so as they sat side by side on her bed, washing their beans down with rum and tap water, he explained, "I think it's left over from the Aztec empire. Most Latins just get as excited as the rest of us when they're looking for a fight. Mexicans with enough Indian in them to show play by a different set of rules. To begin with, you're not supposed to scowl at the guy you're out to pick a fight with. You just smile soft and sleepy at him and murmur sweet things to him."

She swallowed some rum with a puzzled frown and said, "That sounds like a funny way to pick a fight, if you ask me."

"I'm not asking you. Hernan is the bozo we have to look out for. He's got it buzzing around in his empty skull that I made him look bad with Villa. He probably never liked gringos all that much to begin with. So he's likely to start up with us and . . ."

"How did *I* get into your feud with some greaser I've never even met?" she said in a tone of injured innocence.

"You're my adelita, for official purposes. I told the others you were mine to protect you. That was before I knew Hernan had it in for us, and I say *us* because a soldado and his adelita are one, as the game "Tu Madre" is played. Hernan doesn't want to strike the first blow or be first to reach for a weapon. Villa told him not to start up with me."

"Then what have you or, all right, *we* have to worry about?" she asked with an uncertain smile.

He said, "A lot. Hernan will start by spreading the word, behind my back, that I may act like a big shot but that I'm really afraid of him. That'll be the cue for at least one or two born troublemakers to sidle up to me and tip me off that Hernan seems to have it in for me. If I just laugh and say I'm not worried about him, they'll go right back to him with my implied challenge. If I don't say anything they'll think, and say, that I *am* afraid of him."

She suddenly brightened and said, "Oh, we had girls like that at my boarding school. We called them sneaky bitches."

Stringer nodded, "Hernan's not out for a hair pulling contest. He'll try to establish that we're enemies and that I'm naturally the one to blame. To my face he'll smile and sort of flutter his lashes like he's flirting with me. He will be. He'll want me to ask him why he's acting so funny, so that he can say something funny, just short of an open challenge. Spanish is low on curse words. Most of the ones they have, they've picked up from us. But that doesn't mean a Mex can't talk dirty. They just have to put things more subtly. Instead of calling you a bastard, they might offer their respects to your mother, and even your father, if only anyone knew who that passing stranger might have been."

She nodded and said, "Oh, "Tu Madre" means Your Mother, right?"

He grimaced and replied, "Tu Madre is usually the last remark passed before the action starts. The insult's so subtle that the guy who said it can insist, later, that he meant no harm and that you'd just gone loco and attacked him. There's nothing wrong, on the surface, with say asking another gent, with a purr, how his mother is feeling this evening. On the other hand, it's not Spanish Custom to even mention the women of a man's family until and unless he's introduced you to them, see?"

She tried to. She said, "It sounds sort of Islamic, if you ask me. Why can't you just pretend you're Christian and it's all right to ask how someone's momma feels?"

He said, "It *is* Islamic. The Spanish fought the Moors for eight hundred years and picked up lots of odd notions from them. The point is that both sides, and all the others watching, know the rules of the game. You *can* pretend the oily insults aren't getting through to you. You might even avoid a showdown that way. Then you get to start all over with the next bozo who wants to show his stuff. Backing down gringos is a sort of national sport, like bull fighting or highway robbery. Sooner of later, I'll have to stand up for my manhood, if only to keep from doing the dishes for some tough adelita. Meanwhile, guess how you'll be treated as the mujer of a man who shows no balls?"

Bobbie blushed and flustered, "I wish you wouldn't be so crude, Stuart. I'm not used to being spoken to that bluntly!"

He shrugged. "Facts are facts, and we're going to have to face up to them unless you want to be treated crude as hell. By now Hernan should have heard I've claimed your fair white body. Don't look so shocked. Somebody had to. A woman with no male escort is up for grabs among men of Villa's class, and you wouldn't be all that safe from old Diaz, himself."

She said she understood why he'd had to fib about their, ah, relationship.

He washed that down with more rum and muttered, "Why me, Lord? I always thought Sir Galahad was sort of foolish about all those fair maids he got into sword fights over." Then he told her, "In any event, Hernan is as likely to start passing remarks about you as my mother. Either way, I'm supposed to blow my top at him. This siesta gives us until three, four at the latest, before he can get at me. I can likely avoid a showdown the first time around. I don't want you to show yourself outside at all. Everyone knows you're pretty and I might be able to leave the party early by allowing I haven't had all I want, yet."

She gasped and demanded, "Stuart! Is that any way to talk to a lady?"

He said, "Forget you're a lady. We're two Anglos surrounded by a lot of people who'd rather say gringo. Should anyone be looking and you find my arm around your dainty waist, or up your skirts, for that matter, just grit your teeth and consider how much worse things will get if we act like we don't like each other a lot."

She started to cry. He put a reassuring arm around her shaking shoulders and soothed, "I know. It gets worse on the trail if we have to march on with this outfit. No way we can avoid sharing the same sleeping bag and I'm only human. So let's study on how we can get away from here with your chastity intact. I haven't seen any ponies since we took the site. If there's so much as a burro, Villa gets to ride it. Might there be a railroad hand car around here anywhere, and would you know if there was one?"

She shook her head and tried, "There's my bicycle in the store room, if some greaser hasn't stolen it. I didn't know when I brought it along that the roads around here were so dreadful."

He laughed. Then he cocked an eyebrow and asked, "Just one?" to which she replied, "Of course. How many bicycles would I have brought out here to begin with?"

Before he could answer, there was a knock on the locked door and Villa's voice called out, "Hey, Stringer. I'm sorry to spoil your fun, but I need you. Open up."

"Si, si un momento," Stringer answered in a sleepy voice as he sprang from the bed and proceeded to shuck off his jacket and pull his shirt tails out, whispering, "Under the covers! Now!"

When he just had to open the door, Villa was presented with the sight of Stringer putting his gun rig back on as, behind him, Bobbie demurely peered over the edge of the sheets at both of them with her long blond hair in romantic disarray. Villa smiled knowingly and told Stringer, "That telegrafo set in the office keeps clicking. I need you to tell me what the cabrones want."

Stringer followed the chunky Mex the length of the veranda. Villa had been right about the telegraph set on the manager's desk. Stringer sat down, found a pencil and a scrap of paper, and proceeded to decode the dots

and dashes into block letters. He wasn't too skilled at
the craft to begin with and they were naturally sending
in Spanish. When the message began to repeat he
handed the paper across the desk to Villa. The "General" held it upside down as he scowled at it, saying,
"You had better read it for me. I do not have my glasses
on me right now."

Stringer nodded and said, "They just want to know if
anyone on the other side might still be here. They're
sending a troop train, with the cavalry mounts in box
cars. They figure to hit between midnight and dawn.
That leaves us eight or nine hours to make tracks, Pancho."

Villa scowled and asked, "For why would Los Federales wish us to know this in advance? Is a most stupid way to launch an attack, no?"

Stringer suggested, "I don't think the message was
meant for us. They might not think anyone riding with
you knows how to read. I told you those guys I brushed
with looked Anglo. So they're still missing, along with
my blonde who used to be their company nurse. They
have no way of knowing the company guards threw in
with you. They may be hoping someone's still holding
out here and, if so, they don't want them making any
desperate moves with help on the way, right?"

Villa brightened and said, "That works. You say they
got a train and *horses* on the way here? Bueno. Now I
wish for you to send them a message for me."

So Stringer did. He wrote it down and transcribed it
in Morse before he sent it, lest they wonder about his
hesitant hand on the key. Then he wired back that, as
they'd hoped, a couple of company men and a handful
of loyal guards were forted up in the headquarters building, surrounded by drunken savages.

The other side wired back that they should stay put and leave the rest up to Los Federales. Then they asked who they were talking to and Stringer decided that now would be a swell time for the rebels to cut the wire. So he told Villa, "We can't push our luck any further. They're getting nosy." Then he disconnected one of the wires between the set and its battery and added, "You sure are hell on telegraph wires, Pancho."

Villa laughed and said, "No matter. We have plenty of time to set up a nice ambush, no?"

Stringer frowned and replied, "There's no such thing as a *nice* ambush, and we're talking about a cavalry column, damn it!"

Villa nodded and said, "Bueno. I just said I could use the horses and extra guns. They think the company men still hold the compound. So they'll expect to find my army in the bushes all around. When no bushes shoot at them, they should think we have run away. When they ride in to congratulate themselves, I will have them in a grand crossfire. We'd better build some camp fires further out. That will give us good light to shoot by while it makes them think they have driven us off."

"Pancho, you don't have the fire power. You don't have the ponies you'll need when they lick you, this time."

But Villa just looked hurt and asked, "Who said anything about losing? I told you I needed a big win to get back my reputation. Once word gets out that I have beaten a whole army column and have my own train as well, all Chihuahua will rise up to follow me!"

Stringer didn't argue. He got up to leave. "Screw that blonde all you like," Villa told him, "but don't get drunk. We got to start setting things up in five or six hours."

Stringer agreed that sounded about right and left to get back to Bobbie. She was still under the covers. He locked the door again and told her, "There's a military relief column on its way by rail. Villa thinks he can ambush it. I think he's been smoking funny cigarettes. Either way, we can't afford to be here when the shooting starts. Both sides tend to shoot at folk like us from force of habit. We'd better use your bike as soon as it gets dark."

She asked how two people could ride one bicycle. He told her, "It won't be easy, even with you riding the handlebars. The only route smooth enough to matter is that service road alongside the railroad tracks. It figures to be bumpy as hell, but . . ."

"What about that troop train coming the other way?" she cut in.

To which he could only answer, "Don't be so optimistic. We figure to get shot by *this* side long before we have to worry about the *other*, right?"

CHAPTER
ELEVEN

La siesta ended way before dark. Stringer tried staying put in Bobbie's room. But after someone had pounded on the door more than once to tell him they were missing supper, Stringer decided they were attracting more attention holed up than by just going along with the crowd. He told the American girl to stay put, explaining, "I'll be able to get away sooner if I say I have to feed you in bed."

She blushed again and asked, "Oh, whatever will they think of me?"

Stringer smiled and said, "Let's hope they do. Most of them don't know you on sight and your looks have probably improved in the telling. You don't speak the lingo and if you did, the other adelitas would still want to start up with you. Natural brunettes are sort of jealous of blondes. Keep the door locked and if anyone yells through it at you, just keep saying 'No comprendo' 'til they go away. If it's important they'll check with me. We want them to dismiss you as just a lovetoy I got first dibs on, see?"

She said she didn't like that much, but agreed she'd likely get in more trouble where the spiteful greasers, as she called them, could get at her blond hair.

Stringer strapped on his gun, straightened his hat,

and went out to face the music. Someone was strumming "La Cucaracha" again. He saw Hernan near the same barbecue fire as Villa. He decided to join the crowd around another one. He realized he'd made a tactical error when Hernan strolled over to join him, away from Villa's personal supervision. From the looks on the others faces, Stringer knew Hernan had already spread the word. He nodded at Hernan, looking as poker-faced as he could manage. Hernan smiled pleasantly and asked, "Where is the lovely señorita? Doesn't she eat anything but cock?"

Stringer smiled back just as sweetly to reply, "I was just about to take some food to her. This meat smelled fine until just now. But all of a sudden I smell shit. How do you manage to fart with your mouth like that, Hernan?"

The adelita carving the meat giggled. Some of the others dared to smile, not looking at either of them. Hernan could see who'd scored that point. So he tried, "Are you sure you don't have her chained to the bed, my big Don Juan? I find it difficult to believe even a puta would give herself willingly to such an excuse for a man. Maybe I should go over and show her how a real man does it, no?"

Stringer purred back at him, "You sound hard up for a woman. I can see why, seeing neither your sister or you *mother* seem to be with us this evening."

Hernan blanched and almost stopped smiling as he asked in a tone of deadly calm, "Was that my mother I just heard you mention? I reproach you for your manners, Gringo. Did I say anything about your mother, even though everyone knows she is a whore?"

Stringer stepped clear of the fire as everyone but Hernan moved around to the far side with amazing speed and grace. Stringer knew it was his turn. So he said, softly, "I'm willing to call us even if you are. If you're not, feel free to fill your fist."

He was hoping to throw Hernan's timing off by bringing matters to a head earlier in the game than usual. Most guys playing "Tu Madre" liked to work up a full head of steam before they went for broke. But Hernan seemed made of sterner stuff, or he'd already worked up a head of steam. At any rate, he went for his gun.

As the muzzle blast of Stringer's .38 echoed away Hernan just lay there with that same soft smile on his lips and a wet crimson rose pinned to his shirt, just above his crossed cartridge belts. His dead hand still gripped the butt of his .45, but the gun was still in its holster. Stringer just stood there in the sudden silence, his smoking six-gun still in his fist, as he waited to see what happened next.

What happened next was Villa striding over, his own gun out, to politely demand some explanation. The adelita who'd been carving started carving again as she announced, "Was a fair fight, Pancho. Hernan slapped leather first."

Another witness added, "Not fast enough. This Yanqui moves like spit on a hot stove. I have seen some quick draws in my time, but this Yanqui is quicker than quick!"

"Was a fair fight." The girl with the carving knife repeated, adding, "Hernan told me, earlier, to watch him teach the big-shot gringo a good lesson. To tell the truth, I wanted to warn the Yanqui, but was not my place to interfere in the business between men."

Villa put his own gun away, muttering, "I told Hernan not to act so dumb. Now I need a new segundo."

Then he smiled at the American who'd just shot his old
one and said, "Bueno. You were smarter than he was
before he proved how dumb he was. After we finish
eating we got things for to work out, Stringer. What do
you know about high explosives?"

Stringer began to reload as he muttered, "Enough not
to mess with them if I don't have to." But Villa insisted,
"You have to. We found lots of dynamite in the mine up
the hill. Look me up at sunset and we shall see what we
can do about laying some land mines, eh?"

Stringer knew this was no time to argue. So he just
shrugged and as soon as Villa wandered off, he filled a
heaping tin plate of roast whatever and carried it back to
Bobbie.

He told her it was beef. He wanted to be sure he had
her strength up when it come time to make their move.
Her dress was darker than his blue denim outfit. As the
light outside got tricky, he had her lead him to the storeroom on the far side of the building. Her bicycle was
still there. But its red rubber tires were flat. She started
rummaging around for her air pump, making far too
much noise as she turned over boxes. "Never mind,"
Stringer said, "We figure to run over a lot of cactus
anyway. Duck back in your room for now. I'll see if I
can wheel this off a ways without attracting attention,
for now."

She didn't know what he was talking about, but did
as she was told. Stringer was wheeling her bike alone,
as far from her as the river bank, when one of Villas'
men fell in step with him to say, "I've been looking all
over for you. Pancho wants you. What are you doing
with that toy?"

Stringer said, "Toying with it. I just found it in a

storeroom and I thought I'd see if I could ride it up the
river bed a ways."

The guerrilla shrugged and said, "Maybe later, then.
After you see what the general wants, eh?"

So Stringer tossed the bike out of sight and hopefully
out of mind in a clump of chamis and legged it back to
the main building he'd just come from, with the alert
but unsuspecting Mex rambling on about blowing up
federales.

They found Villa and some of the others seated in the
veranda steps with a couple of boxes of dynamite and
similar views on Los Federales. Villa pouted as he said,
"Haven't you had enough of that gringa, yet? We got to
string some fuses, Amigo. They ought to dismount out
on the edge of the site and sneak in on foot. So, if we
place charges in a big circle, and wire them to one mag-
neto plunger..."

"You'll make a lot of noise and waste a lot of dynamite." Stringer cut in, explaining, "You want to get at
least some of the leaders and rattle the rest with your
first blast. Once it gets noisy, troops hit the dirt and tend
to stay there 'til someone tells them different. That's
when your men have the best chance of mopping them
up. If I were you, I'd put that dynamite, all of it, under
this building."

"Blow up my own headquarters?" Villa asked in an
injured tone.

Stringer said, "You won't need a headquarters here if
you get your hands on all those ponies and extra guns.
But you just proved my point. This is the most impor-
tant-looking strong point around here. Los Federales
will be expecting to find the company personnel or, failing that, you, holed up here. They'll call out a few
times and then, getting no answer, they'll storm it.

When they find nobody home they'll make it *their* headquarters at least long enough to repair that telegraph set and . . ."

"Ay, carramba!" Villa cut in, "When I become El Presidente, you get to be Secretary of War! I love it! We shall station our women way up slope and dig the men in closer. I think I better post an arson squad to set fire to the water tower when this building goes on its journey to the sky and then . . ."

"You're the boss." Stringer cut in with a casual yawn. Then he said, "I have to get my gringa and our bedding to a safer place. I'll see you around the battle, sometime, maybe."

Then he mounted the steps and strolled the veranda back to Bobbie's room, forgotten for the moment, as Villa started to issue his new orders. He joined the girl in her darkening room and told her, "I think we're set. Get that canteen from your wardrobe and fill it with tap water. Tap as much water into yourself as you can while you're at it. I'll roll the bedding."

He wrapped just the top padded quilt and one wool blanket around the rifle, binding everything together with shoe laces Bobbie wouldn't be needing. Then he joined her in the bath and forced himself to swallow five glasses of water. She didn't ask why when he shoved the half-used roll of toilet paper in a jacket pocket. They scooped up other possibles to stuff in his pockets and he told her to put on her sun bonnet. Then he said, "Bueno. Now we're going to walk, not run, and let me do the talking."

But nobody challenged them as he strolled away into the gathering dusk with her and his modest load. They got to where he'd cached her bike. He looked around, saw it was too dark now to notice anyone else and, hoping that worked both ways, lashed the bundle to the bike frame and wheeled it down into the river bed. The mud had barely dried hard enough to walk and wheel across. He manhandled it up the far bank and told her to follow Indian file as he bulled it east through the chaparral a quarter mile. Then he swung toward the railroad line and when they got to the service road, he stomped his heels a few times and then said, "Well, asphalt paving would be better. But what the hell. Hoist your skirts and perch your sweet rump on the handlebars."

She didn't want to expose her stockings. But she didn't want her skirts tangled in the spokes any more than Stringer did. So once he had her in position, he gave a good shove and forked himself aboard behind her.

Thanks to the soft tires, he was able to more or less follow one dust-filled wagon rut without shaking them up too much. Ahead of him on the handlebars, Bobbie asked, "What's that clinking below us? Might something be wrong with my chain?" To which he replied with a wry chuckle, "Those are my spurs you hear. I don't usually wear them riding a bike."

She giggled and said she felt awfully silly, riding like this. He asked, "How do you think I feel? This is a girl's bike."

They both laughed like hell and that got them down the road a piece before his legs began to notice what a chore he'd set them. Bobbie tried to be a sport about her behind, seeing he was working hardest to save it, but after about an hour she insisted that she had to rest it just a minute. So he stopped, let her off, but they kept walking as he wheeled the bike between them. He said, "Every little step helps when you're running for your life. I doubt we're ten miles out, yet and we want to be a heap further when we're missed.

She asked how far they had to go. He said, "Hell, I don't even know where we're going. The map puts us a good eighty miles from the nearest jerkwater town on the main line to Juarez. It's just after nine P.M. now. If we can average ten miles an hour we ought to make it just after dawn."

She protested, "Oh, Stuart, I just can't ride those handlebars that far! I'm sure I'm already bruised black and blue on my you-know-what."

He said, "If you're not, I can promise you will be. Get back on. Bruises don't hurt half as much as bullet holes and we've got us some desert to cross."

The next hour's ride felt as bad as he'd expected. Stringer was cramping leg muscles he'd never suspected he owned. In hopes of distracting himself, and Bobbie as well, he mused aloud, "This reminds of my first cattle drive, when I was six or eight. I'd been riding my own pony on the home spread since I was old enough to walk, of course. But that had been kid stuff. My Uncle Don warned me his market drive to Sacramento called for more serious riding. But you know how kids are. The first day on the trail was fun. Next morning I was too stiff and saddlesore to mount up. But I did. I had to. I knew the other hands would think I was a baby if I didn't act like a man."

She protested, "But you *were* a baby, Stuart. Surely your own uncle should have understood you were still a little boy."

He ignored a shooting pain along the top of one thigh as he replied, "He'd warned me not to tag along unless I was up to a man's job. My Uncle Don was and still is one of the most decent gents I've ever know. But he takes herding cows serious and leaves baby notions to the women folk. I knew he and the other hands riding with us had ridden further, through rain and snow and Indians. The hell of it was, I knew they *would* understand if a little kid like me couldn't keep up with them. That was why I just had to keep up with them. I confess I cried some, riding drag where the dust hid my face. By the end of that second day, I could barely stand up and I was sure I'd be crippled for life. But when the camp cook handed me a plate of beans and asked me how I was holding up, I managed to allow the cowboy life had going to school beat by miles."

"I can't say as much for riding double across Chihuahua in the dark," Bobbie murmured, "How did you ever manage to survive the next day's drive, Stuart?"

He grunted, "I managed. Hurting is sort of like hunger. After a spell you get sort of used to it. It's the first few days that convinces you you'll surely die. Since I was still alive, I saw there was little sense brooding about it and, later that day, when a snake-spooked yearling busted loose to throw its fool self into a canyon, it was me who headed it off just in time. I can still remember how I felt when my uncle caught up, stared at me sort of curious, and told me I'd done right."

He pumped the pedals harder as he added, "I felt *almost*, but not quite, as proud the first time I saw my own byline in print above a news feature I'd had published.

"You must be very fond of your Uncle Don."

"I have to be. He's kin. But that wasn't what made me feel so good when he praised me. He praised me as one grown man praises another. I knew I'd never be a baby no more. And by the time the drive was over, I'd taught my kid's body to do as I damn well told it to. Our bodies act sissy on us, if we let them. They try to protect themselves from our will power by starting to hurt long before we've done 'em any real damage."

They hit a bump and she gasped, "Oh, Lord, I wish you were the one in charge of my poor derriere!"

He chuckled, slyly, and said, "So do I." and that seemed to shut her up as she rode on with her naked thighs spread open to the desert breezes. She knew better than to mention what the handle bar bolt was doing to her.

They fell into a routine of walking a few hundred paces and riding a lot farther, covering, they hoped, the ten miles an hour they needed. Stretching their legs helped some. They were getting more used to the pain when, a little before midnight, they saw a glimmer of light on the horizon ahead. She asked if that could be a house.

"More like that troop train I told you about. We'd best take a little stroll into the chaparral."

So they did. They were flattened out with her bike in the sand with a nice clump of cactus between them and the tracks as the troop train thundered by. He knew they were safe, but as the earth throbbed under them Bobbie seemed out to climb inside his duds with him, sobbing in terror. He held her tight and kissed her trembling lips. It seemed the natural thing to do, and she didn't seem to mind, judging by the way she kissed back as the window lights of the troop train swept across the cactus pads above them. As the danger passed on by, it was Bobbie who first noticed where his free hand had wandered, without conscious direction on his part. She stiffened and grabbed his wrist, then she relaxed in his arms with a sigh of surrender and murmured, "You will be gentle, won't you? It's been quite a while and . . ."

"Hold the thought." He cut in, patting the object of his affection a reluctant adios as he explained, "We're going to need all our strength before morning and I'm bushed as hell as it is."

She wouldn't talk to him after that as they rode on for the next hour or so. He didn't really mind. His distracted genitals helped him ignore the cramps in his legs and the thought that he'd blown that chance forever made him sore enough to peddle harder.

But Bobbie broke her silence when they both heard a distant roll of thunder and she gasped, "Oh, no! That's all we need, a desert cloudburst!"

"That was dynamite," he grunted, and stopped to cock his ear to the darkness. He could barely make out the soft rustle of the now very distant small arms fire. He told her, "We'd best walk on a piece while we have the time. I'd say both sides are sort of busy back there, now."

He filled her in on Villa's planned ambush as he wheeled the bike between them for about a quarter-mile. She asked who he thought might be winning back there. "*¿Quien sabe?*" Stringer shrugged, "Maybe the army, maybe Villa, maybe nobody. I don't expect them to settle the matter one way or the other for years. Diaz is too tough to be overthrown. But Diaz can't live forever and God knows what'll happen once he's gone."

She asked if he thought Villa would ever wind up running Mexico. He shook his head and said, "He's too innocent to hold the top job. Tougher, or let's say, smarter gents may use him to grab the job for themselves. Politics are played sort of like king of the mountain down here. Once they get rid of Diaz, they'll start knocking each other off, and I, for one, don't aim to be here when they hold the elections with bullets. So let's see if we can get to the main line while the trains are still running sort of regular. The one thing you've always had to give Diaz is that he's made the trains run by the posted timetables."

But along about four in the morning, while Bobbie and Stringer were still out in the middle of nowhere, they heard the troop train coming back. This time the headlight of the locomotive was a lot brighter when Stringer heard the rumble and glanced back over his shoulder. "Hang on!" he said, and rode them off the road into the brush a ways before they spilled in the sand and he dragged Bobbie and the bike behind some tumbleweed piled against the twisty trunk of a mesquite tree, growling, "Keep your head down. This is way too close but it'll have to do, I hope."

The train was rolling slower, now, as if the hand on the throttle was uncertain, or as if the troops on board were looking closer at the passing scenery. "Oh, Stuart, I'm so frightened," she moaned.

He told her that made two of them as he drew his .38 with one hand and held her flat in the sand with the other. He didn't know what good either gesture would really do if they were spotted, but he had to do something. "The army must have won." She whispered, "Maybe, if we tell them we're Americans instead of bandits . . ."

"Don't bet on it," he told her, adding, "The official policy of the Diaz Dictatorship is to make nice-nice with El Gringo. But good help is hard to find, and all bets are off when the army or rurales get the chance to pick up some quick cash or, hell, even a pair of boots."

He didn't say what the hired guns of the so-called friendly government would do to a good-looking woman of any race if they got the chance. She was already scared enough.

Then, above the rumble of the casually rolling train, they heard the singing. Male and female voices, a lot of them, were belting out "La Cucaracha" as the train rolled past their hiding place. As the train rolled safely by, Stringer chuckled and said, "I guess that tells us who won. Don't ask me how." Then he kissed her again.

She responded in kind, but murmured, "Please, Stuart, don't start anything you don't mean to finish." Then she gasped and added, "Oh! Good heavens! With my underpants on?"

He put a few more friendly strokes into her before he said, "You're right. Let's strip down and do this right."

So they did, but as he spread her naked beneath the desert stars she murmured, "Oh, this is lovely, darling. But what was that you said about conserving our strength?"

He growled, "That was when I still thought we had some place sensible to get to. Villa can't roll that train he just captured up and down the main line until he takes the railroad town I thought we were headed for. Meanwhile, it's still cool enough to do this and, God knows, we may never get another chance."

So she wrapped her pale thighs around his bare waist in passionate agreement and they forgot about the rest of the world for an all too brief period in heaven.

When at last they had to pause for breath, Stringer told her, "Hold the thought and save my place. We've got to find a safer spot to spread our bedding, and if you're a good little girl I'll even let you catch some sleep before the sun bakes us too hot for anything but cussing."

So she picked up her clothing to follow him in her knee socks and high buttons a half mile from the tracks, and as they lay down atop the bedding she was very good indeed. So he didn't try to think about the coming dawn. It figured to be just awful no matter how you sliced it.

They actually managed to sleep some time after sunrise before the hot rays of the desert sun found them snuggled naked among the shielding cactus to give them a good spanking. As they sat up, sleepy-eyed but already uncomfortable in the harsh glare, Bobbie covered her naked breasts with her forearms and gasped, "Oh, heavens, I feel so embarrassed! Don't look at me, Stuart!"

He handed her her dress, muttering, "I'd already figured you were blond all over. But we don't want to get sunburned."

As she dressed facing away from him, he found their one canteen, unscrewed it, and held it out to her, saying, "Take it easy on the agua. I've got to find us better shade, as soon as I find my damned boots."

He hauled on the rest of his duds while he was at it and got to his feet for a look-see all around. There was nothing to see for miles but cactus and chaparral. The padded quilt was pink and blue. The wool blanket was deep maroon. He'd never seen a clump of maroon cactus or greaswood. But all colors ran together in desert sunlight. So they'd have to chance it. A day on the desert without shade was the most obvious danger for miles. So he spread the quilt closer to the cactus and draped the wool blanket over the spiney pads to form an improvised tent. Bobbie didn't need to be told twice to crawl under it, but she said it still felt stuffy. He helped himself to some canteen water and crawled into the meager shade with her, saying, "It'll get a lot hotter in the sun before it gets cooler."

She stared at him wide-eyed and asked, "Do you mean we're stuck here until sunset, with only one canteen full of water?"

He said, "It's not full, now. But that's the least of our worries. In a pinch we can refill it with cactus juice. It sure ain't lemonade. It'll make you sick if you drink too much on an empty stomach. But it's better than dying of thirst."

He began to roll a smoke, sitting cross-legged in their tiny patch of shade, as he mused half to himself, "I was with a posse searching for lost greenhorns one time. We found them dead on the desert, poor fools. They'd died of thirst surrounded by many a barrel cactus. Barrel cactus juice is almost pure water, too."

She said, "I'm not thirsty right now. I'm *hungry!*"

He said, "I know. That's why I'm rolling us this smoke. It takes weeks to starve to death, as long as you have water. It helps a mite if you smoke between meals."

She said she didn't smoke. That chewed up some time for them and by the time he had her puffing away she got to giggle and say there seemed to be no end to the naughty habits he was out to introduce her to.

Then she had to spoil it all by asking where they'd go as soon as it was dark again. He grimaced and said, "I'm working on that. That train ride to Juarez and points north doesn't look so good now. With Villa and Los Federales enjoying a running gun fight up and down the main line, we're going to have to look for another way home."

She protested, "Riding double on my poor bicycle?

We must be hundreds of miles south of the border, Stuart!"

He nodded and said he'd noticed. He said, "I make it more like three hundred and change, as the crow flies, and that contraption ain't no crow. There's no road to follow, and even if there was, it would be crawling with rebels and rurales, now that Villa's raised so much hell. Our best bet might be cross country, away from the few roads, on foot."

She protested she could never hike across three hundred miles of desert in high button shoes. He pointed out that she'd never know for sure before she tried. Then he said, "Stretch out and try for some shut-eye. I'll wake you up if the sun ever goes down around here."

It took her an hour of bitching to fall into a fitful doze. He was about to join her when he heard something. It had sounded like brush popping against leather.

He reached for the rifle and crawled out into the sunlight. It felt like crawling across the floor of a brick kiln with the firebox lit. When he finally felt safe to take off his hat and stick his head up through some mesquite leaves he saw he'd been right. Two riders had left the service road to investigate the patch of maroon wool they'd spotted off to one side, the sharp-eyed sons of bitches.

They were paid to ride sharp-eyed. Nobody wore those big gray sombreros and matching charro outfits but Los Rurales. They had to be patrolling out from the main rail line, so that meant Villa had gone somewhere else with the captured train. Stringer knew they were supposed to be searching for Mex outlaws, not lost Anglo visitors. But as he'd told Bobbie, such uncouth lawmen, no more than licensed bandits in their own right, might not know just who they were after at times like these.

As he watched, still uncertain what to do next, the rurales dismounted, tethered their ponies, and hauled out their saddle guns to move in on the mysterious patch of wool, afoot. Then Bobbie solved Stringer's moral quandry by rising from the not too distant shade to wave and call out, "Yoo hoo, officers?" and damned near got her head blown off.

But as both rurales moved as one to throw down on the blonde with their carbines, Stringer blew the farthest one away with a rifle shot and the closer one naturally pegged a shot at him instead of the girl.

The rattled rurale missed. Stringer didn't. From the way that big sombrero soared skyward Stringer knew he'd nailed the bastard with a spine shot. The other one was still moaning for his mother as Stringer moved in fast to finish him off with his third round. He was still standing there when Bobbie ran over to join him, demanding, "Have you gone crazy? They were policemen!"

He said, "I noticed. They didn't give a damn who *we* were. We have to get out of these parts, *poco tiempo*. These guys come in bunches and the buzzards will be pinpointing these two any minute."

She gasped and turned to head back to their bike and bedding. He said, "Not that way, damn it. Their horses are over yonder, and they carry plenty of water and trail provisions with them."

But even as he led her over to the tethered government mounts she kept moaning that if he wanted her opinion, they were already in enough trouble. He boosted her aboard the bay and handed her the reins. Then he untethered the pinto and mounted beside her before he took time to explain, "We're already in as much trouble with the law as we can get. The law down here is worse than Villa and his rebels and by now *he's* sore at us and it's safe to assume every hand will be turned against us between here and the Land of the Free. There's nothing like a little trip through other parts to make you realize just how good that sounds, whether you took it serious or not when the teacher made you salute the Stars and Stripes every morning, right?"

"Oh, get me back to my own country again and I swear I'll never make fun of my dear old teachers again!" she sobbed.

They found a mesquite-shaded arroyo two hours north of the seldom-used tracks and holed up just in time to save the ponies and probably themselves from sunstroke. When Bobbie asked how he could be sure they were safe he told her, "There's no such thing as safe in Chihuahua right now. But even the desert sidewinders avoid the noonday sun and there's a lot of that all around. Watch where you squat to drop it in the bushes down here, though."

She assured him her ass was reserved for his abuse alone, so they spent the lazy afternoon abusing each other while the ponies broused mesquite pods and watered on the cactus pads Stringer peeled for them. He remembered what Villa had said about darkness and the Yaqui. He didn't consult the already worried blonde about the odds. He decided on his own that army and police patrols were the greater risk, right now. The Yaqui should stay holed up in the hills if they had a lick of sense, and desert nights were cool as well as concealing. So they traveled mostly at night after that first mad dash away from the scene of their brush with rurales, then got to detour a lot as they circled wide of any night lights they spotted now and again in the distance.

As they worked their way ever closer to the border and safety, the girl naturally bitched louder and more often about her discomfort and what she called his crudity. He thought he was just being considerate. There was just no way two people could travel under such intimate terms and pretend nobody ever had to take a crap. He couldn't shave, she couldn't douche and their duds were glazed and stinky by the time he allowed they were close enough to the border to risk a late afternoon dash for the same. She was sure they were lost and it hadn't occured to either of them to make love in the heat and dust of the last arroyo he'd chosen. So he said she was free to stay there if she liked, and of course she tagged along, muttering mean things about crude cowboys out to get her lost forever in a trackless wilderness.

But when they topped a rise to spy the wreckage of that border grandstand in the sunset light, and he told her what it was, she brightened and asked how on earth he'd managed to find the way without anything like a trail to follow. He said, "It wasn't easy. Keep a tight grip on your reins. The ground ahead's pockmarked by shell craters, and ponies spook when they catch a whiff of stale human meat."

But while both their mounts did roll their eyes and act skittish on their way across the now ominously silent battlefield, they saw no actual bodies. The victorious federales had been neater than usual, with others watching from a grandstand.

The U.S. Army had recoiled its concertina wire and policed up its own spent brass. The stands had been half carted away by locals salvaging lumber in a land where lumber was expensive. Bobbie had been swearing all the way that as soon as they crossed the border she meant to dismount and kiss the sacred soil of the U.S. of A., but as they forged on toward town in the gloaming she contented herself with running a pocket comb through her hair and pinning it neater under her sunbonnet, protesting that she was in no condition to be seen in public, even in the dark.

It was more like twilight when they rode at last into the once more sleepy little town of Columbus. A few lights were burning, but otherwise the place looked deserted. The local economy had reverted to one saloon and the one hotel by the railroad stop was open and anxious for business. The old lady behind the hotel desk was so happy to see them that she insisted they take the honeymoon suite, with bath, for one dollar, or seventy-five cents in advance. Stringer placed a silver cartwheel on the fake marble counter between them and scrawled something noncommital on the open register as he said he noticed business seemed slow. The old landlady sniffed and said, "You can say that again. We was thinking of closing until roundup time. That big show they promised us was a total bust. You heard about the battle they put on just across the border, of course?"

He allowed they'd heard talk about some Mexicans arranging to fight a battle or something and she sniffed and said, "We got gypped. After all the fanfare all anyone got to see was a lot of smoke and dust for less than a full hour. Then it was over and all the dudes cleared out, mighty let down. Who ever heard of a battle lasting less than an hour?"

Stringer told her that he'd heard Little Big Horn had lasted more like twenty minutes and led Bobbie upstairs. He told her he'd be back as soon as he checked in with the local law. She was already streaking for the bathroom. He shrugged and left her there to freshen up.

He led the two ponies afoot up the dusty street to the town lockup. He tethered them out front and strode in. The old lawman he'd found so helpful before looked up from behind the desk, shot a glance at the wall clock, and said, "Evening, Stringer. We was about to close up for the night. You sure look dusty. Been out on the desert all this time?"

Stringer nodded and said, "Yep. I got two ponies out front I thought I'd best talk over with you. They're wearing Mex government brands and packing rurale saddles. I found them down Mexico way. You'd know better than me what the proper form of disposing of 'em might be."

The old-timer smiled thinly and said, "Possession is nine tenths of the law as far as Mex stock goes in these parts. You aim to keep 'em or sell 'em?"

Stringer smiled uncertainly and replied, "Can't keep 'em. I got a train to catch."

The town law got up from his desk, saying, "I'd best have a look at 'em, then. I runs the town livery on the side, and you won't get a better deal off anyone else in town. I got your old gladstone bag around here somewheres, by the way. Them French friends of your'n left your baggage in my safekeeping when they left town in that fancy private car. They seemed sort of pissed by the results of that battle they come all this way to take moving pictures of. I can't say it looked like much to me, even though I'm more used to Mex revolutions. Did you watch it, old son?"

Stringer followed the old-timer out front, muttering, "I did. From where I was watching I saw more dust and gunsmoke than anything else."

The old-timer agreed he'd seen a better show at Shiloh, then he stepped off the walk to examine the two horses, observing, "Well, they sure need currycombing, and I doubt they've tasted oats since they was foaled, but they're both lessn' four years old and the bay has some Spanish barb in her. How does four bits sound to you, saddles and bridles throwed in, of course?"

Fifty dollars was a lot more than Stringer had paid for them. So he said, "Done," slapped the old man's held-out palm, and asked, "When does the next train pass through?"

The town law reached for his wallet as he said, "There's an eastbound due any minute. The next west-bound rolls in closer to ten this evening. That's the one you'll want to take back to the coast, right?"

Stringer agreed. As the old-timer counted out fifty dollars in paper and silver coinage Stringer casually asked how the bounty deal on that hired gun, Jones, had gone. The old man chuckled and said, "I just now gave you some of it. Lucky for me, the reward poster read dead or alive. The son of a bitch died on us in his cell, the next night after you gave him to us."

Stringer blinked in surprise and asked, "He died? What in thunder might have possessed him to do a thing like that?"

"Pizen," said the town law, in an unconcerned tone, adding, "The doc said the symptoms read morphinous. He must not have cottoned to the notion of death by hanging."

"You mean he poisoned his fool self?" asked Stringer. To which the old-timer answered in an injured tone, "It sure wasn't *us* as slipped the stuff to him. He had no visitors and we all et the same chop suey from the Chinee joint up the street that night. He likely had the stuff hid on him in the lining of his duds, or somewhere. The doc said it was an easy way to go. None of us out front heard him going. He just lay dead on his bunk, come breakfast time. I fail to see why you should look so unsettled, MacKail. Nobody can say *you* done it."

Stringer put the money from the horse deal away as he said, "I was sort of wondering who might have sent him after me. I told you, before, someone tried to strand me in the Colorado Desert with that French film crew and, when that failed to work, they sent Jones to do me personal. I'd sort of like to know why."

As they went back inside for his gladstone the east-bound train rolled in, just down the way. The old law-man proposed, "Maybe someone didn't want you covering the story of that battle. Did you notice anything unusual about it?"

Stringer shook his head and said, "Nope, and I surely saw more of it than most. You say the Pathe crew rode out, safe and sound, with the whole thing on film?"

The old-timer hauled Stringer's gladstone out of a wardrobe and handed it to him as he nodded and said, "Yep. Nobody hung around once the smoke had cleared to reveal no more than dusty Mex troopers loading dusty bodies aboard dusty wagons. There was a couple of other moving picture crews who were just as disgusted, as I recall. One of the boys from that L.A. outfit told me over to the saloon, that the whole thing had been a big bust, with nothing recorded on film but blurry shapes dashing hither and yon in clouds of dust. You sure you didn't wind up with a more sinister news angle?"

Stringer shook his head and said, "The one thing I am sure of is that Pancho Villa wants his name in the papers, and I had no idea Los Federales meant to butt in before they did."

They both went back outside so the old lawman could lock up and lead his new stock up to his livery stable. As they shook hands to part friendly, the town law said, "Villa's getting famous, true enough. Word just come in that he got licked again, near some railroad town down yonder. Last anyone heard, he was streaking for Texas again with Los Federales on his tail. If you ask me, that boy ain't never going to amount to much until he learns not to bite off more than he can chew. They're going to kill him one of these days. You just mark my words."

Stringer did, then he trudged his gladstone to the one saloon open in town between exciting occasions, humming "La Cucaracha" under his breath. The old-timer was likely right. But if they didn't kill him, Villa would rise again, and again, until the big shots learned to treat his people better.

In the saloon he ordered a tall cold beer and didn't blame the suspicious barkeep for asking him to pay in advance. He could see in the mirror behind the bar that he looked like a hobo who'd just been thrown off the train when it stopped to jerk water. He needed time to think as much as he needed the beer, as good as it tasted after all that cactus juice. He knew that while his trip across the desert with Bobbie hardly qualified as a ship-board romance, they were getting to that awkward point where she was probably wondering, too, just why they'd said and done all those nice things with nothing much in common but the fact that one was concave where the other was convex and there'd been nobody else to talk to.

They called winding up like that with a gal you

worked with or roomed with at the same boarding house propinquity. He knew better than to throw a term like that at a gal who hadn't really finished high school before she'd decided she was a nurse. He didn't know what he *was* going to tell the poor little gal. Women got men to promise the damndest things in a bedroll, with the desert stars smiling down so infernally romantic.

But he knew it wasn't going to help if he showed up sloshed, so he downed the last of the beer, picked up his gladstone, and went back to the hotel to face the tears and recriminations like a man who had 'em coming.

But when he got there, the old lady behind the desk stopped him, waving an envelope with the hotel's address printed on it, to tell him, "That young lady left this for you, sir. She said she had to catch a train and, land's sake, I hardly recognised her after a bath and a brush-up."

Stringer allowed he could use the same and carried Bobbie's message up to their hired room to read it as he ran himself a hot tub. As he tore the envelope open he wondered where she'd been packing her own money. He'd explored her pretty good and one of the things he'd been most worried about had been how he might persuade her to take the money from the horse sale without insisting she hadn't, damn it, been doing it for money.

He had to wonder, wryly, who'd been most guilty of what when she even used the word propinquity and then added insult to injury by explaining it to *him*. He couldn't have written a better brush-off himself, and he was glad he hadn't been stuck with the chore, for her letter was just as awkward and larded with self justification. He balled it up and threw it in the wastebasket, then he had a long soak and gave himself a good clean shave. He caught himself looking sort of sad-eyed in the mirror as he wiped the last of the lather off, chuckled, and told his reflection, "Well, hell, I guess I got a right to feel a mite let down, now that I don't have to feel like a dirty dog. How was I to know she was such a good sport as well as a great lay? So now I'm all squeaky clean with a double bed at my disposal, and the only gal I know in town has lit out for Ohio!"

CHAPTER
TWELVE

The timing mechanism in Stringer's skull had been thrown out of gear by all that night riding, so he was having a breakfast of salt peanuts and beer in the club car as his train rolled the last weary miles into the L.A. yards. Up forward, the porters would still be trying to get the Pullman passengers awake and dressed for public view by the time they got to the end of the line. A familiar figure with world-weary eyes and a shoulder rig bulging under the suit he had on entered the club car, spotted Stringer seated at his corner table in the early morning light, and came over to join him without pausing at the bar.

"Morning, MacKail," he said, "If I had a drink every time I made her back to this end of the train I'd wind up drunk as a skunk on duty. You may not remember me, but . . ."

"You're Doug Fraser, our clans fought side by side at the Battle of Culloden Moor." Stringer cut in, adding, "I was never allowed to forget things like that. The Mac-Beans were on our other flank, as my grandfather used to recall. He couldn't have been there, either. You still riding shotgun for the S.P. Line, Doug?"

The railroad dick sat down, saying, "I am. It's gotten back to the usual moll molesters and baggage thieves since all that excitement over Columbus way. To what do we owe the honor of your riding our scenic line in duller times, Pard?"

Stringer explained he'd been sent to Columbus to cover the entertaining battle and had gotten sidetracked. As he went on to bring Fraser up to date on his recent adventures, as he noticed the railroad dick was commencing to look uncomfortable as a hound dog shitting on the church steps. He paused to sip some beer. Then he asked why.

Fraser stared out at the greaswood and telegraph poles whipping by as he muttered, "You got me in sort of a bind. Us rare highlanders are supposed to stick together. But you do still write for the newspaper, don't you?"

Stringer nodded dubiously and said, "I don't think I've been fired for failing to file a story on what everyone there agrees they found a dusty disappointment. Are you hinting you've got news that ain't fit to print, Doug?"

The railroad dick said, "Not if I want to hold on to my own job. But I might be able to save you a ride out to Western Avenue all fired up, if you'd like to give your word that none of what I tell you ever happened, officially, that is."

Stringer raised a cautious eyebrow to say, "Stranding folk on the desert and then sending hired guns when that failed to finish them hardly rates a cover-up by honest men, Doug."

Fraser nodded and said, "I know. You're adding two and two to get five or six. Your word this conversation never took place on company time, MacKail?"

Stringer figured he could go along with that. So he nodded and Fraser leaned closer to tell him, "That

French outfit, Pathe News, offered to sue the Southern Pacific flat broke for the way they wound up routed so odd on the S.P. tracks. So I was one of the boys Mister Huntington personally assigned to the case. A yard boss and some brakemen who don't work for S.P. no more owned up to having been bribed by a certain rival motion picture outfit to make sure Pathe got there too late. Nothing was said about killing anybody. The Pathe crew was just supposed to get lost for a spell, see?"

Stringer nodded soberly and said, "I was with 'em. I got them to Columbus in time, even if the battle wasn't all that thrilling on film in the end. But sending that hired gun after me hardly qualifies as a two reel comedy, Doug."

Fraser nodded and said, "I knew Jones by rep. I'm pleased as Punch to hear he's out of business at last. His business was pure assassination, for big money. Way more than those railroaders ever got. Aside from which, no Hollywoodland wiseass had any motive for doing you in, once Pathe had made it all the way to Columbus, right?"

Stringer muttered, "I liked it the other way better. Try her this way. I had words with your yard boss when his first move was an attempt to shunt that Pathe car to San Diego. I figured out how to get us off that deserted desert spur as well. Whether the film company who corrupted them knew that or not, they must have known I suspected they'd been corrupted, so . . ."

"Wrong tree," the railroad dick cut in, explaining, "One of the things that made Mister Huntington so mad was that those bums had sold out so cheap. That hired gun didn't work for drinking money. Jones wouldn't have even frowned at you for less than four figures, cash in advance. So whoever sent *him* after you was serious as hell about your demise. You'd know better than me who might want you shut up, about what."

Stringer thanked the railroad dick for his words of cheer and Fraser got back up to make sure nobody got off at the end of the line with the wrong baggage.

As the train rolled past some shacks on the outskirts of the sprawling city, Stringer considered his own baggage under the table. He'd naturally packed his six-gun away with his shaving kit and such before boarding in Columbus. L.A. was getting too sissy these days, for a man to wander about dressed up for Dodge. He wasn't up to explaining he'd come west to be a motion picture cowboy star when, not if, some copper badge inquired as to his intent in the crowded Union Depot. In any case, it seemed hardly likely anyone would be laying for him as he changed trains. He had to be arriving unexpectedly, since he hadn't known he'd be aboard this particular train, himself, before he'd boarded it clean over in New Mexico Territory.

On the other hand, it was always better to be safe than sorry. He made room for his gladstone on the table, opened it, and took out only his .38, shutting the holster and gunbelt away again.

He made sure the double-action hammer still rode on an empty chamber, leaving five in the wheel for real, and shoved the cold muzzle down the front of his jeans. With his denim jacket buttoned down the front he could likely pass for slightly pregnant.

He must have, judging from some of the odd looks he got as he got off at the end of the line in his faded cow duds and beat-up Stetson. These days folk in L.A. were more used to wooly chaps and ten gallon hats, it seemed.

Feeling slightly foolish, Stringer headed for the platforms where one caught the Frisco Coaster, packing his gladstone in his left hand and scanning the bustling crowd for signs of murderous intent. A railroad redcap fell in step beside him, offering to take charge of his bag. Stringer shook his head and said, "It's not that heavy and I'm almost there." By this time he was moving up the cement in line with the waiting coaster and only needed to find an infernal set of open steps to climb aboard the train. He saw the others were boarding a few cars up, where a pestiferous conductor was making them show their tickets before he'd let them pass.

A couple of young gals were walking in step just ahead of him and the fool redcap, who tagged along behind him. Their skirts parted like the Red Sea as they moved on past a gent who was just standing there. As their eyes met, Stringer knew. And the son of a bitch already had his gun coming out from under his long travel duster!

The redcap pushed Stringer into the narrow slot between two passenger coaches, but it was still close. A bullet spanged off metal as Stringer rolled under the coupled platforms without taking time to think. There wasn't time to think, as all hell broke loose on the far side of the train. Stringer rose in the gloom between his train and the next one over, gun in hand, to see yet another redcap facing him down at the far end. The railroad worker's hands were empty and he seemed to be waving Stringer his way. So Stringer went on, numbly wondering, as he got a mite closer, when they'd started hiring orientals instead of colored gents as baggage smashers.

The mysterious redcap yelled, "Behind you!" Stringer whirled about, landing on one knee in the grit, just in time to peg an unaimed shot at the bastard aiming

at him with a Colt Dragoon. Whether by luck or instinct, Stringer sat the would-be back-shooter on his ass
with a dead-center hit just above the heart. Then he was
up again and running after the redcap, who certainly had
to have a better notion than he did where they were
going.

His mysterious guide slowed to a more sedate albeit
still brisk walk as they moved through the crowded
depot. They got a lot of odd looks until Stringer thought
to stuff his smoking gun back in his pants. Behind
them, police whistles were chirping but no more guns
seemed to be going off right now. When they wound up
on the walk out front, the redcap shoved Stringer into a
horsedrawn cab, gladstone and all, and the cab lit out
like it was on its way to a fire before Stringer had time
to sit up and look around.

When he could see where they were going, they
seemed to be in Chinatown. The one in L.A. was small,
so they only swung a few corners and then they were in
an odd-smelling alley, where the driver told him curtly
to get out, then left him standing there as he went cruis-
ing for another fare.

Stringer stood there staring absently about until a tin
door opened and yet another mysterious oriental hissed
him inside. It was dark and someone had been burning
sandalwood in hopes of disguising the smell of opium.
It hadn't worked. The guide he could barely make out
led Stringer up a dark staircase. When Stringer asked
where they were going, he got no answer, so he hauled
out his gun again. A sliding door opened and he found
himself alone with a mighty pretty Chinese lady in a
more brightly-lit and handsomely furnished upstairs
room, if one's taste ran to blood-red drapes and gold
wallpaper with all the low-slung furniture polished with

India ink. The gal was dressed in red silk and she'd apparently combed her hair with India ink as well. She sat down on a low red cushioned divan and patted him to a seat by her side, saying, "You may call me Chin Chin if you like. The true name of my tong is of no more importance among friends."

Stringer stayed on his feet but lowered the muzzle of his .38 to a politer position as he smiled down at her uncertainly and said, "I sure don't want to be your enemy. Your hatchet men are pretty good. But to what do I owe this honor, ma'am?"

She stared soberly up at him with her warm sloe eyes as she told him, "To your own honor, of course. There was nothing to be gained and, as you now know, a lot for you to lose when you published that story about certain San Francisco real estate moguls wanting to move our people to the Hunter's Point mudflats as a civic improvement. Why did you write that, Stuart MacKail? What had my people ever done for you that you should risk your own life for them?"

He shrugged modestly and said, "Well, nobody in Chinatown ever did me harm, and it seemed just plain dirty to evict folk out to those mudflats just so greedy landlords could get even richer. I didn't know I was risking my life. I wasn't out to be a hero. I was only reporting the simple truth. That's gotten me in trouble before. But it goes with the job, and I can take care of myself."

She shook her head firmly and said, "They have your boarding house on Rincon Hill staked out, too. Or they will have until dark. Our hatchet men, as you call them, prefer to work with less light on the subject. They did what they had to at the depot just now, because simple men like you are as hard to find as lavender jade, and more valuable. The evil man who wanted to have you killed has just died of a mysterious illness his doctors have no name for. But before we could get to him, he'd sent his running dogs out on your trail. It may take us a few days to make sure of every one. Meanwhile, you will be safe here with me, until all of your enemies have been eliminated."

He smiled crookedly and said, "I'm beginning to. They told me in Columbus that Jones enjoyed some *chop suey* in his jail cell just before he passed away so mysteriously. How big a tong might we be talking about, Miss Chin Chin?"

She smiled softly and said, "Bigger than some think. I am not at liberty to confirm or deny suspicions about cowtown chop suey, save to assure you that you won't be served any *here*. We've never understood why your people order it."

He laughed and said, "Ignorance of your ways, I reckon. I've learned to like real Cantonese cooking just fine and, come to study on it, I only had a few peanuts for breakfast."

She nodded and said, "In that case, allow me to order you a breakfast fit for an honored guest. My orders are to see to all your comforts and do my best to make sure your stay with me is all a man might desire."

Stringer put his gun away and she sure did. The food and drink he was served in bed for the next few days was as fine as any he'd ever had, although not half as spicy as Chin Chin herself was.